DAN SMITH

2 PALMER STREET, FROME, SOMERSET BA11 1DS

First published in Great Britain in 2018
Chicken House
2 Palmer Street
Frome, Somerset BA11 1DS
United Kingdom
www.chickenhousebooks.com

Cover and interior design by Steve Wells
Typeset by Dorchester Typesetting Group Ltd
Printed and bound in Great Britain by CPI Group (UK) Ltd, Croydon, CR0 4YY

The paper used in this Chicken House book is made from wood grown in sustainable forests.

1 3 5 7 9 10 8 6 4 2

British Library Cataloguing in Publication data available.

PB ISBN 978-1-910655-92-4
eISBN 978-1-911077-55-8

For Carolyn,
who helped me get from there to here.

Also by Dan Smith

Big Game

Boy X

My Brother's Secret

My Friend the Enemy

OUTPOST ZERO, ANTARCTICA
3 DAYS AGO

There was something happening at Outpost Zero. Something that wasn't *supposed* to be happening, and Sofia Diaz wanted to get to the bottom of it.

Curiosity killed the cat, she thought as she throttled the engine and accelerated across the ice. *Yeah, well. Satisfaction brought it back.* And the only thing that was going to satisfy Sofia Diaz was finding out exactly what those BioMesa guys were doing at The Chasm.

Outpost Zero was run by the Exodus Project, and was supposed to be just thirty-two people – eight families – training for a life on Mars. Sofia had been in Antarctica with her mum and dad, and her brother Pablo, for two months now. Two months without sunlight because she had persuaded her family to join the Exodus Project. But a few weeks after Sofia and the other seven families arrived at the base, some new guys turned up. Eight of them, working for a research company called BioMesa – but their work didn't have anything to do with Mars or the Exodus Project. They had come to Antarctica because of The Chasm – a huge crack that had appeared in the ice several months ago, not far from Outpost Zero. And Sofia wanted to know *exactly* what they were up to, but when they were in the main part of the base – The Hub – the BioMesa guys kept themselves to themselves, and when Sofia asked the other families about them, she was met with blank faces and gently shaking heads.

'Don't ask,' everyone said. 'Just pretend they're not here.'

But they *were* there, wearing their bright red Outpost Zero jackets, with the black BioMesa logo on the sleeve instead of an Exodus Project badge like everyone else. And they left at the same time every morning to ride out to The Chasm, and they came back at the same time every evening. Except for yesterday. Yesterday, they came back three hours later than usual, and when Sofia asked where they had been, everyone clammed up and told her not to ask.

At fourteen years old, Sofia was the youngest member on base, and she was expected to do as she was told. But Sofia hardly ever did what was expected, and *never* did as she was told, so she waited until the BioMesa guys had returned to the base, before hurrying back to her room. On her way there, she bumped into a young, bearded man with the name 'Jennings' printed on the chest of his blue BioMesa sweater. He was coming back from the kitchen area, carrying a mug of coffee.

'No harm done,' he flicked the splash of coffee from his hand and smiled.

He seemed nice, and Sofia almost felt guilty for bumping into him.

Almost.

In her bedroom, Sofia felt a nervous thrill of excitement as she pulled on her Extreme Cold Weather gear. She slipped out through the emergency exit at the end of the West Tunnel, jumped down on to the ice, and sneaked round to the Arctic Cat snowmobiles parked at the front of Outpost Zero. Sofia chose the furthest snowmobile, and pushed it away from the base. As soon as she was out of earshot, she started the engine.

No one saw or heard her leave.

Soon the base became nothing more than a few glittering lights behind her. With a surge of adrenaline, Sofia kept going until the dim red glow of the beacons came into view. They marked the BioMesa research area. When she arrived, Sofia switched off the snowmobile and pulled Jennings' access card from her pocket. She approached a door that was built into the towering ice wall in front of her.

Too easy, she smiled to herself. *He'll think he lost it in the snow.*

She wiped ice from the scanner on the door, and

touched the card against it.

The door slid open and Sofia stepped inside.

Now let's see what you guys have been up to.

She followed a tunnel down to a square cavern in the ice. The right side of the giant room was home to a bank of computers. The left side, close to where Sofia was standing, was latticed with a grid of rectangular holes cut into the ground.

Like graves, she thought. *Cold graves.*

At the far end of the cavern, the world dropped away to never-ending darkness. The Chasm. This wasn't the first time Sofia had seen The Chasm, but something about it drew her towards the edge. She wanted to know what was in its hidden depths. As she came closer, though, she glanced into the nearest grave and saw something that made her stop.

It was filled with long ice cores; cylinders drilled from deep below the surface. They were the kind of thing scientists got nerdy about when they were researching climate change. Boring stuff, as far as Sofia was concerned, except the cores in *this* grave were different from the cores in all the others.

Something was frozen inside them.

Sofia got down on all fours and lifted out the nearest core. It was inside a clear plastic tube with the BioMesa logo, and '#31' printed on the side. She twisted it this way and that, but all she could see were dark shapes about the size of the tip of her thumb, stuck inside the ice. There was one close to the end. So close, in fact, that a little bit of scraping with a sharp instrument might . . . just . . . ease it out . . . Sofia took off one of her clumsy gloves and fished a Gerber scout knife from her pocket. She flicked open the blade and used it to pop open the seal on the tube. She slid out the core and scraped at the ice until the small black object was protruding from the end of the core. Sofia used her fingers to loosen it and pull it free.

She held it in the palm of her hand and inspected her treasure.

It was actually more brown than black. And now she could see it better, she thought it looked like a cocoon. Or a pupa – the kind of thing a beetle would grow inside. It was cold against the skin on the palm of her hand, but the longer she held it, the more she had the sense that it was growing warm.

And when it moved, Sofia jumped so suddenly she almost dropped it.

Her heart was thumping, her blood rushing in her ears, and she held her hand further away from her face, as if something was about to burst from the pupa and . . .

And what? It's tiny. What could it do? Don't be such a scaredy-cat.

She smiled to herself and slipped the object into her pocket. She'd take it back and show Doc Blair; he'd find out what it was. In fact, why not take the whole ice core back to Doc Blair? There was something strange going on here, and it wasn't cool that BioMesa was keeping secrets from the people living on the base. It was not cool at all. The others needed to know about this.

Sofia slipped the ice core back into its container and made her way to the door. Outside, she put the plastic tube on the back of the Arctic Cat, pulled her goggles over her eyes, and started the engine.

As she accelerated across the snow towards the lights of Outpost Zero, Sofia thought about the grave filled with ice cores, and wondered if the BioMesa people would notice one was missing. But the more she thought about it, the less she cared. What could they do? She wasn't scared of them.

But she *would* be scared.

Later.

She would be scared to death.

APPROACHING OUTPOST ZERO, ANTARCTICA
NOW

The DHC-6 Twin Otter aircraft lurched and rattled with a violent sensation of falling that startled Zak from his book. He had been trying to lose himself in the adventure story in front of him, but it was becoming harder and harder as they flew further into the storm.

Everything about the plane was 'no-frills' and rickety. Half the interior was lined with fold-down seats – six on either side, facing each other – and the rest was filled with steel cargo containers secured with nylon webbing straps. The exposed metal walls and floor were freezing to the touch.

The plane shook again, dropping in the thin air, and Zak's

heart dropped with it. Cold and fear were all he could feel now. His hands were shaking so much there was no point trying to read. Even the latest Jackson Jones adventure couldn't take his mind off it, so he closed his book and stared at the cover.

Jackson Jones and the Ghosts of the Antarctic.

In the picture, two brave adventurers were standing in front of a jagged cave cut into a wall of ice. One of the adventurers was Jackson Jones himself; wearing a heavy orange parka similar to the one Zak was wearing right now. Jackson was also dressed in black windproof trousers, and had a black hood over his head. He was stepping back in surprise, with one arm raised, brandishing a vicious ice axe. Following close behind was a boy dressed the same. The cave was dark, with a clawed hand gripping one side of it, as if something was about to leap out. From the black shadows inside, a pair of glowing red eyes glared at the approaching adventurers. But Jackson Jones and his companion weren't afraid. Jackson Jones was never afraid – something Zak Reeves wished he could say about himself.

Zak held the book flat and jammed both hands between his knees.

The ancient aircraft carried just five of them, including the pilot – the only five people crazy enough to be flying out to Antarctica in the middle of the worst storm in years.

Sitting opposite, Zak's sister May was also holding a book – one of those relationship books she always read – but Zak could tell she wasn't concentrating on it. She looked ill at the best of times, with all the pale make-up and black eyeliner she liked to wear, but she looked even worse right now. The colour had drained from her face and her brow was scrunched into a deep scowl. Resting on her thigh, the index and middle fingers of her right hand were crossed.

May was fifteen – three years older than Zak – and she was one of those kids at school who was proud to be different. 'Why fit in when you can stand out?' she always said. May liked to wear black. In fact, she *loved* to wear black. Black jeans (ripped, of course), black T-shirt with either a band logo or a picture from a horror film on it, and a black leather jacket. She had three piercings in each ear – Mum wouldn't let her have her nose or lip pierced – and she darkened her eyes with thick eyeliner. Her black hair usually hung down and hid most of her face, and she could scowl like a champion. May called herself an 'emo-punk-half-Chinese-horror-fan', and she was unlike anybody else at West Allen School; she 'customized' her uniform with badges, covered her books in pictures cut from horror film magazines, and carried a backpack with *The Evil Dead* printed on it. She had a handful of friends but most of the other kids thought she was weird, and kept out of her way. One girl in particular was just plain mean because May wasn't like her and her friends. Vanessa Morton-Chandler said nasty things to May and spread rumours behind her back. May usually just made some kind of sarcastic remark, gave Vanessa a withering look and did a good job of pretending it didn't bother her, but Zak knew it hurt her when they were unkind. That's why the black clothes and the leather were important to May; they were her armour.

Zak would never admit it to her, but he thought his sister was cool.

When she caught sight of him watching her, May brushed away the wisps of straight black hair falling over her dark eyes. She tightened her bow-shaped mouth and nodded once.

Beside her, Dad took off his glasses and winked at Zak. 'You OK, my young Padawan?' The words came out as a wispy cloud of warm breath in the cold air. 'Quite an adventure we're having, eh?' He pinched the bridge of his nose, then put his glasses back on. 'And we haven't even got there yet. You'll have a good story to tell your friends when you get back.'

'I'd rather tell them about the sun in St Lucia,' May said. 'Can't we just turn around and–'

'We come up on it now.' The pilot's thick Russian accent crackled over the intercom system. 'You will be seeing Outpost Zero at any moment.'

The plane shook again and Zak gritted his teeth, trying not to think about dying. He'd had enough of thinking about that, and he was sick of it. It would be kind of funny, though, if after everything the doctors had said, he ended up dying in a plane crash. Funny strange, that is, not funny ha ha. It wasn't supposed to happen like that; all of them dying together in some kind of horrible accident. It was supposed to be just *him*, slowly fading away in a hospital bed, the disease eating away at his brain. Zak was supposed to leave *them* behind, so he was sure that today they were all going to be fine. It was just turbulence. In a storm. Over Antarctica. No problem. Nothing to worry about.

Yeah, right.

He glanced at Mum, sitting beside him with her lips clamped so tight it made the tiny zigzag scar just below her nose go white. The scar had come from the time she fell off her bike when she was growing up in Hong Kong – Zak had heard the story a million times – and when it went white, it was always a dead giveaway that she was either worried or annoyed. The usual twinkle in her brown eyes was dull too, and when she smoothed her dark hair back from her narrow face, she forced a smile at him. 'Be there soon.'

Zak turned to watch through the window behind him. On the other side of the small circle of glass, the propeller was a blur. Beyond that, there was nothing. Just black. No light at all. Zak knew that when the sun had dipped below the horizon at Outpost Zero three weeks ago, the people who lived there were prepared for a long night. It would be *months* before the sun would rise again. If the sky was clear, Zak guessed there would have been stars, but for now the storm smothered everything.

Dad had told Zak that Outpost Zero was in a natural dent in the landscape – like the top of a long-dead volcano. It was a kind of a shallow bowl, with low mountains to the west and a wall of ice to the east, before the world dropped away into The Chasm. But from what Zak could see, they might as well have been over London – or Mars, for that matter – because there was nothing to see but black. Or, as May would say, there was *literally* nothing to see but black.

'We are heading down,' the pilot said. 'Into the storm. It will be bumpy. Ve-ry bumpy.' As soon as the words left his mouth, the aircraft lurched to one side and dropped.

Zak's insides squashed up into his chest, and his bum lifted away from the torn padding of the seat. The safety belt dug into his waist, keeping him from tumbling into the cabin, then he thumped back down as the whole plane shook like a washing machine on full spin.

'You see.' Dima laughed. 'What I tell you? Bumpy!'

Yeah, hilarious, Zak thought as the plane dropped once more, juddering in the storm.

We're not *going to crash,* he told himself. *We're NOT going to crash. This isn't how it happens. I don't die like this. Please don't crash.*

A picture flashed in his mind, of him in a hospital bed, eyes closed and at peace. Mum and Dad and May were standing around him. Grandma and Grandad in the background. *That* was how he was supposed to die.

Dima's accented words came over the intercom once more. 'Don't worry.' He shifted in his seat to see back through the open cockpit door. 'The Reeves family will be safe tonight. I get the Reeves family to Outpost Zero in one piece, OK?' He was slightly overweight, with a mop of dark hair, greying at the temples. His face was weather-beaten, and his nose was crooked from the many times he had broken it. 'You not worry. I have landed in much worse than this. Much worse. One time, total white-out on the ground. I see nothing at all. *Da*, it was a bad landing, plane could not be used again, but everything was *horror show*.'

Horror show? And the plane couldn't be used again? How bad is this going to be? Zak stared at the pilot. *The guy is completely nuts.*

'I pulling your leg.' Dima's face broke into a huge tobacco-stained smile with a tooth missing at the top. 'It's a joke. *No one* can land in total white-out, not even me. Impossible to see.'

Oh. Great. Zak turned back to the window as lightning crackled in the sky. He caught a glimpse of brooding clouds hanging heavy, but it was what lay below that scared him the most. A swirling mass of ice and snow that hammered against the plane as it descended.

If that wasn't a total white-out, Zak didn't know what was.

'Don't listen to him, Zak.' Mum put a reassuring hand on his arm. 'We're going to be fine.' And she did that thing where her expression was so full of concern her face crumpled up like a piece of paper. 'You feeling OK?'

'Yeah, fine.' He moved his arm, pretending to rearrange the collar of his thick coat, but really it was just to get Mum's hand off him. Sometimes, sympathy is the worst thing in the world.

'You see the base now?' Dima's voice carried into the cabin once more. 'The lights. Look.' He pointed out the front of the cockpit but all Zak could see was Dima's wonky reflection in the glass, so he shifted his focus to see beyond it, and there it was. An orangey glow filtering through the storm.

'Outpost Zero,' Dima said. 'The base. At last we are arriving.'

The glow became more concentrated as they approached, and before long, Zak could make out individual lights, and he began to think this wasn't a total white-out after all. One thing was for sure, though – the base was smaller than he had expected.

In the cockpit, Dima was speaking into his communication system as he took the plane down. 'Outpost Zero, Twin Otter seven-one-five request advisory.'

The storm blustered, scooping the plane from side to side as Dima dipped the nose, angling to the left of the main Outpost Zero lights. He lowered his voice so it was impossible to hear what he was saying over the comms, but he was frantically flipping switches, checking read-outs, and tapping dials like something was bothering him.

Like something was wrong.

Zak's stomach cramped when he realized what it was. There weren't any runway lights. Nothing. No sign of a landing strip at all. Maybe this *was* how he was going to die. Forget about doctors and drips and treatments. Forget about hospital beds with clean white sheets, fading away, and everyone being sad he was gone. They *were* all going to die together. They were going to hit the base and die in a blazing fireball, or–

Lightning flashed outside, bright and white, filling the cabin. There was the sound of shearing metal and the engines screamed.

'It's OK.' Dima glanced back. 'Don't worry. We be OK. Everything will be *horror show.*'

That expression again. *Horror show.*

'Shouldn't the landing strip be lit up?' Dad shouted.

'They . . . there is no answer from the base.' Dima flicked more switches. 'Perhaps it is the weather.'

'And the lights?' Dad asked.

'I have done this many times. I know this runway like I know the back parts of my own hands; we will be A-OK. With Outpost Zero lights on, I know where the landing strip is, so–'

The base lights went out.

One moment Outpost Zero was there, glowing like a beacon, and the next it was gone. All the buildings went dark. There was nothing to see through the cockpit window but the swirling whiteness of an Antarctic blizzard.

'Damn it!' Dima abandoned the switches and concentrated on lifting the nose of the plane. He needed to take them back up again. Fast.

The twin engines whined in protest and Zak slipped sideways in his seat as the aircraft made a steep and terrifying climb. It rose high through the storm, rattling and shaking like a shopping trolley with a wonky wheel. Zak locked eyes with his sister and gripped his book so hard his fingertips throbbed and his knuckles popped.

I'm not going to die. Not here. Not like this.

His mum put an arm around his shoulder, and although his instinct was to shrug it away, like always, he accepted it, let her leave it there.

'We'll be fine,' she said, but she was trembling and Zak knew she was as scared as he was. Even more scared, probably. Death was coming for Zak anyway. Every day, every hour, every minute brought it a step closer. Sometimes he thought about nothing else. It was difficult not to when everyone kept reminding him of it. Everyone trying to be so *nice* all the time.

'What the hell is going on?' Dad said. 'Why did they turn the lights out?'

Dima didn't reply; he was too focused on controlling the plane, fighting the sudden climb and the angry weather. And as soon as the aircraft began to level out, and the engines stopped protesting, he was on his comms again, trying to contact the base. 'Outpost Zero, Twin Otter seven-one-five request advisory. Please respond.' He tapped the right ear cup of his headset and tried again. 'Outpost Zero, Twin Otter seven-one-five request advisory. Please respond. *Respond*.'

'Anything?' Dad asked. 'Are you getting anything?'

Dima swore in Russian and tore off the headset, throwing it down beside him. He cursed again and glanced back with an expression Zak didn't like. Not one bit.

'Well?' Dad asked.

'I . . . please. Everything is A-OK. I guess they have some kind of power problem.'

'You guess?'

'I mean, that must be what it is. A power problem.' He took a deep breath and retrieved his headset.

'So what now?' Mum asked as Dima took the plane into

a wide circle. 'Does this mean we have to go back?'

'Not possible. I *have* to land here. For fuel.'

'What?' May's eyes widened and she leant forward, still crossing her fingers. 'Are you saying there's only enough fuel to go one way? We don't have enough to get back? What kind of stupid plane is this?'

'We refuel at Outpost Zero.'

'Yeah, if you can *land*. Except you can't, can you? You can't see anything. How can you land in this?' She turned to Mum and Dad. 'I mean, *literally*, how can he land in this?'

Dad shared a look with Mum.

'No, seriously.' May was becoming more agitated. 'How can he land when he can't even see the runway? What are our chances of making it? We're going to be–'

'May,' Mum cut her short.

'We can land anywhere,' Dima said. 'Here the ground is mostly flat and we have polar camping gear and survival supplies if we need them. I have landed here many times. It is fine. I promise. Whatever happens, we be A-OK.'

Zak could tell he was trying to sound confident, but he heard the doubt in Dima's voice and saw the worry in his eyes. The pilot was just as afraid as the rest of them.

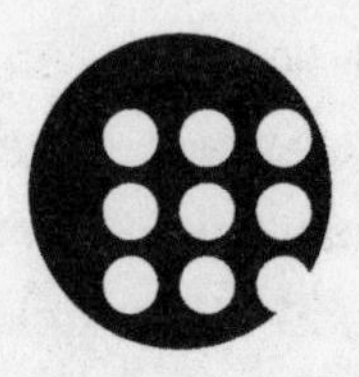

OUTPOST ZERO, ANTARCTICA
21 HOURS AGO

The blizzard tore at Sofia's coat as she staggered across the ice. She fixed her eyes on the metal staircase leading up to Outpost Zero, and prayed she would reach it. She didn't want to end up like the others.

Those stairs were her lifeline. The Outpost was the only place for her to go. Everything else was a swirling frenzy of wind and snow and ice, spinning in never-ending clouds. It howled around her, clawing under her hood, sapping her strength.

Just a bit further. That's all. A bit further and she would be safe from–

Tick-tack-tick-tack. Tick-tack-tick-tack.

Her thoughts blazed white with terror at the sound.

Tick-tack-tick-tack.

They were coming for her.

Sofia forced herself onwards, reaching the stairs and grabbing the handrail to drag herself up. At the top, she lunged for the panel on the wall beside the door. She fumbled her gloved fingers under the handle and yanked it open with a violent tug that unbalanced her.

'*Help me*.' Prof Peters' last words echoed in her ears as she steadied herself and grabbed the emergency lever. She pulled it hard to one side. With a calm hiss, the Outpost door slid open and she was there. She was home free.

Sofia scrambled to safety and turned to punch the button. She hit it hard, the door immediately beginning to slide shut. As it did so, she backed away, staring at the horror approaching through the blizzard.

The world was lost in the nightmare of swirling ice and howling wind, but there were shapes out there. Dreadful shapes in the storm.

The door took an eternity to close. Sofia willed it to move faster, and when it eventually slid shut, she engaged the lock and her legs gave in. Her knees buckled and she sank to the floor, staring at the door. Outpost Zero was silent except for the muffled sound of the storm raging outside. Sofia tried not to think about what she had seen – about what had happened to the others. Prof Peters, Commander Miller, Dr Asan, Lee, Doc Blair . . . *all* of them.

But this wasn't over yet. There was one more thing she had to do.

She drew on her last reserves of strength and pulled herself to her feet. It wasn't far to Refuge, and that's where she needed to go. It was essential she upload the video. When the Exodus Project sent a rescue party, the footage might – just *might* – save someone's life.

OUTPOST ZERO, ANTARCTICA
NOW

Engines whined. Alarms screamed. Warnings lights blinked.

Staring through the cockpit window, Zak couldn't tear his eyes from the swirling void as they descended into the storm. The plane shuddered and rattled. It dropped and buffeted, lurching to the side. Zak tightened his grip and clenched his teeth as he wished for a miracle. If only Dima could see the landing strip. If only the lights would–

A sudden intense pain flashed in his head as if a hot spear had pierced his right eye. It exploded in his mind and blossomed like black fire. He'd had pains before – a symptom of his condition – but never anything as awful as this. This wasn't just a physical pain; it felt *alive*. His breath faltered, his eyes squeezed shut, and he *was* the pain. That's *all* he was. There was nothing in his mind but a vast black sea of pain.

And then it let go. The fiery grip relaxed and his thoughts returned to what had been running through his mind before the attack. He had been wishing for a miracle . . . for the lights to come back on.

'Brace!' Dima was shouting. 'Everybody brace! The ground is coming up on us. We're going to–'

Zak opened his eyes and the lights at Outpost Zero burst into life. In an instant, the main building lit up like a beacon, and bright beams chased along the length of the landing strip as they ignited one by one.

'Thank God!' Dima said under his breath.

The storm continued to shake the plane like it was in one of the snow globes Grandma sent May every Christmas from Hong Kong. It reeled from side to side, the wings tilting first one way then the other. Zak's stomach churned with every sudden movement of the aircraft. His adrenaline spiked with every shudder and rattle, but Dima held it on course as he took them down. There was an awful grinding from beneath the fuselage as the skis lowered into place, and a few seconds later they touched the ice with a heavy crunch.

As the Russian pilot slowed the engines and brought the plane sliding to a standstill, nobody spoke. Zak supposed they were grateful to be in one piece. May's crossed fingers must have brought them luck.

Dima sighed and took off his headset. He rolled his neck from side to side and turned to his passengers. 'Welcome to Outpost Zero,' he said. 'Welcome to the Exodus Project. The outside temperature is minus forty degrees Celsius, your pilot's name is Dimitri Alekseyevich Milanov, and he is as relieved as you are to be on the ground. I hope you had a pleasant flight and that you will fly Dima Airways again in the future.'

'I don't think so,' May muttered under her breath.

'Well done, Dima.' Dad's voice was shaky and he had to clear his throat. He took off his glasses and pinched the bridge of his nose as he collected his thoughts. 'Let's get everyone inside, shall we?'

Zak unclipped his seat belt with trembling hands and turned to the window. He stared through the storm at the orange glow of lights. It looked strange out there; nothing but white and orange and–

The lights went out across Outpost Zero. The landing lights, the windows, everything. The base plunged into darkness.

'What's going on now?' Dad said, but Zak took no notice of him because exactly as everything went out again, he saw something move out there. Something large among the flickers of ice and snow. A black shape passing along the length of the plane.

'What's that?' He pressed his face closer to the window, peering left and right.

'What's what?' May asked.

'I dunno. Something . . . Hey, you don't get polar bears here, do you?'

'Polar bears?' May had recovered from being close to death and was unbuckling her seat belt. 'That's the *North* Pole, doofus. We're south. In fact, we're about as far away from the North Pole as you can get, you freak.'

Yep, she had *definitely* recovered.

'I know,' Zak said. 'But I'm pretty sure I just saw–'

'The only animals out there are penguins.' She came to stand beside him, pressing her face close to his as she looked out. 'Nothing else. You know, this is the only place in the world that doesn't have spiders – unless you count those horrible drones Mum and Dad built.'

'What about all those creepy things we saw online? Sea spiders and worms and things? All those freaky creatures with too many legs.'

'They're in the sea. Duh.'

Zak pulled a face at her. 'I knew there was a reason why you're my favourite sister.'

'Lucky for you, I'm your *only* sister.'

'Lucky for you too,' Zak said. 'You get me all to yourself.' She was being moody, but Zak could hardly blame her. They weren't supposed to be here, in a place that didn't see daylight for months on end. They were *supposed* to be in sunny St Lucia, lying on a beach, which was where they had been two days ago. Two weeks of relaxing family time before . . . well, before Zak's treatment. The doctors said it would be unpleasant – the treatment, that is, not the holiday in St Lucia – but Zak had a feeling it was going to be a whole lot worse than 'unpleasant'.

'Ugh,' May complained. 'Whose stupid idea was it to come here?' She glared at Zak.

'What? It wasn't *my* idea.'

'Yeah it was. When Mum and Dad got that call about their stupid Spider things, they weren't going to come. Because of your . . . thing.' She tapped her head. 'But *you* persuaded them.'

'They wouldn't have come if they didn't want to,' Zak said. 'No one *ever* does what I want. No one ever listens to me.'

'That is *so* not true. We're here because you *said* we should come. And *everything* is about you.'

The *actual* reason for coming to Outpost Zero was for Mum and Dad to fix a problem with the Spider drones they'd built for the Exodus Project. A couple of years ago, when the Spiders were the only thing Mum and Dad talked about, May used to say they probably wished they had drones at home instead of kids. That was before C-Day, though, the day they found out about Zak's condition. Since then, everything *was* about Zak, or rather, it was about 'what's best for Zak'.

When the call came from the Exodus Project, saying the Spiders were malfunctioning, Zak knew Mum and Dad were frustrated. They wanted to give him one awesome, memorable holiday before his treatment began, but they also wanted to take care of their drones. The way Zak saw it, Mum and Dad wanted to fix him, but couldn't. But they *could* fix the drones, so he persuaded them to come. He told them it was a chance for him to see the thing everyone was talking about. The first mission to colonize Mars. They wouldn't be there for longer than a couple of days, he argued, and the base had doctors and equipment, so what harm could it do?

Oh yeah, and there was *another* reason why he told them to come; something a bit more selfish. Outpost Zero was the closest base to The Chasm – a huge rift that had opened up in the Antarctic ice. It was two hundred kilometres long, and at least fifteen kilometres deep. Zak thought it would be just about the most amazing thing he could ever see. A bottomless rip in the Earth. Imagine that. He was far more interested in what might be down there than what might be on Mars, and he was hoping he might have the chance to see it. That way, he could have a real, *proper* adventure at the end of the world.

'I'm sorry,' May said.

'Hm?'

'About what I just said. That everything's about you. It was mean.'

Zak sighed. 'Don't worry, I'm used to it.'

'Hey, I'm not mean *all* the time.'

'No,' Zak said. 'Not *all* the time. Just most of it.'

May gave him a sarcastic smile and moved away. 'I still don't see why Zak and I couldn't have stayed in St Lucia.' Saying it loud enough for everyone to hear, she glared at the floor, getting the expression right before turning it on Mum.

'Do you seriously think we'd have left you there on your own?' Mum said. 'A fifteen-year-old and a twelve-year-old?

And Zak's not well, remember.'

Zak hated it when she talked like that; like he was some kind of invalid. The brilliant thing about May was that she didn't try to wrap him up in cotton wool. May was just as moody with him now as she had always been.

'I'm old enough to be responsible.' May thought twice about the scowl, and softened it to a more vulnerable expression. 'You and Dad could have come on your own. It's not fair we have to–'

'I don't want to hear it. We've been through this enough. And Zak wanted to come, remember.' Mum switched off her cell phone and stuffed it into her coat pocket. 'I guess we're out of reception area now.'

'But really,' May went on. 'You even got a message to say everything was sorted. Your Spiders are fine. They don't even need you here; we could have turned around and gone back to St Lucia and–'

'We were already at the South Shetland Islands,' Mum stopped her. 'It made sense to keep going.'

'It was supposed to be a *holiday*.' May sighed harder than she needed to. 'When do we *ever* get a holiday? You and Dad are always so busy with your stupid drones, and then Zak–'

'Enough.' Mum fixed May with one of her looks. 'We're here now. Anyway, this'll be interesting for you. How many other people can say they've been to Outpost Zero?'

'Oh, I dunno, thirty-two?' May said. 'All of them *families*, training to spend the rest of their lives on Mars. I mean where do they *find* these people? They must be mad.

Who'd want to take their kids to Mars for, like, *for ever.*' She rolled her eyes at Zak, making him smile.

'Actually, it's a few more than thirty-two.' Dad had unbuckled his seat belt and was stretching his back. 'Mum and I have been here, remember. Other scientists too. And the people here aren't mad; they're highly intelligent, highly qualified, and highly trained. Even their kids are well above average.'

'No hope for me and Zak, then.'

'Think about it,' Dad said. 'They're like the early pioneers in America. They're going to find a new way to live. Eventually we're going to use up all our resources on Earth and we'll need somewhere new. The Exodus Project is about finding a way for humanity to survive beyond the small planet we live on. This is just the beginning.'

'Maybe we should be thinking about ways to live on our own planet without destroying it,' May mumbled. 'Anyway, I still think they're mad.'

Zak didn't want to listen to them argue any more, so he pulled up his hood, zipped his coat higher, and tucked his chin into the lining. They'd had to buy Extreme Cold Weather gear on the way here. The coat was a little too big, but he liked the way it smelt. New and fresh.

'So,' Dima climbed through into the main cabin, 'everybody is in one piece?' Without waiting for a reply, he made his way along the plane and opened the door, flooding the aircraft with freezing air.

The others followed, but Zak's legs felt as if they were made of rubber, and he stumbled.

'You all right?' Mum took his arm.

'Fine.' He forced himself not to pull away because he didn't want to hurt Mum's feelings.

'Dizzy? If you get any more headaches, you must–'

'I'm fine. Honest. Why does no one ever listen to me?' He wanted her to stop babying him so he had to show he was strong. With a little more force than necessary, he grabbed his backpack, slung it over his shoulder, and headed for the door.

The tiny hairs inside Zak's nose prickled when he took his first breath of Antarctic air, and the cold tightened the skin on his face. It made him feel more alive than he had felt for weeks.

Dad was the first on to the runway, turning round to offer Zak a hand.

A month ago, Zak would have taken it, but now he didn't want to show any sign of weakness. 'I'm fine,' he said, ignoring Dad's hand and jumping down.

Zak stood on the compacted snow and stared out into the swirling storm.

'Makes you feel like Scott of the Antarctic, doesn't it?' Dad shouted over the howling wind.

'Not exactly.'

'Didn't he, like, die?' May yelled as she jumped down behind them. 'And everyone else who was with him? Starvation and exposure, wasn't it?'

'May-Ling.' You knew she was being warned when Mum used May's Sunday name.

'What?' May said. 'It's true.'

'Well, maybe this isn't the best time to hear about it,' Mum told her.

'Yeah, *May-Ling*,' Zak shouted, and gave his sister a wicked smile.

'Whatever, freak.' May stuck out her tongue at Zak and pulled on her goggles.

'Quite the adventure story, though, eh? Scott, I mean.' Dad wasn't bothered by May's grumpiness. He was used to it.

'Yeah.' Zak crossed his arms over his chest. 'I guess.'

'Anyway, nothing like that would happen now.' Dad leant close to Zak's ear so he didn't have to shout so loud. 'This place has everything you could possibly need. Food, light, warmth–'

'Light?' May said. 'I can't see any light. Everything's switched off.'

'– and there are experts here who would put your doctors to shame. Some amazing equipment too.'

'No welcoming committee, though,' Mum said. 'You think they know we're here?' She pulled her hood tighter as the wind tried to rip it away.

'Maybe we are not welcome,' Dima shouted. A nervous smile wrinkled the saggy skin under his eyes. 'I am joking, of course. Come on, we see what is going on.' He jumped on to the ice and closed the door. 'I leave the plane lights on to help us.'

In the weak glow from the Twin Otter's windows, and keeping together for warmth and safety, they trudged towards the cluster of buildings. The blizzard battered them, rushing beneath their hoods and forcing its way into their coats, but they leant into the wind and battled on towards the place where they were to be stranded.

Alone.

In their own cold, dark, nightmare.

OUTPOST ZERO, ANTARCTICA
NOW

The main building of Outpost Zero was a two-storey module called The Hub. Smaller buildings – containing sleeping quarters and workspaces – were connected to it by tunnels. Sturdy legs kept the base raised a couple of metres above the ice, protecting it from snowdrifts. The whole place was designed to withstand temperatures as low as minus one hundred degrees Celsius, and survive storms that could batter it for weeks.

Zak and the others headed straight for The Hub, seeing it loom out of the swirling blizzard. There was no movement from the base, no light, no sign of life – something that puzzled Zak because he knew there wasn't anywhere for the inhabitants to go. The nearest place was the British Antarctic Survey research station Halley VI, more than five hundred kilometres away.

The wind moaned around the base like a mournful ghost. It battered the new arrivals as they approached, and tiny fragments of ice bombarded them from all directions. Zak was glad he had goggles, otherwise he was sure he would have lost his eyes – if they hadn't already frozen solid in his skull.

A few metres to the right, the Martian Rover Vehicle – the MRV – was parked between The Hub and the runway. It wasn't much more than a silhouette in the storm, but Zak knew it was big, with six huge tyres and a cabin like the cockpit of the *Millennium Falcon* from *Star Wars*. Even as big as it was, it still rocked from side to side in the strong blizzard, creaking and complaining.

As they passed the MRV, a dull ache pulsed in Zak's head as if something was pushing into his thoughts. The feeling of hard ice beneath his boots disappeared and he had the strange impression he was floating in the storm. The MRV was gone. The base too. He was hanging over a vast and swirling black sea that was calling to him, enticing him to fall into its depths. He stared down into its endless darkness, his thoughts spinning and . . . in an instant he was back on the ice, jolting with the sudden sense of falling he sometimes had when he was drifting off to sleep. The base and the MRV were back – exactly where they were supposed to be – but there was something else;

something out of place.

A huge white bear, far bigger than anything he had ever seen in a picture or in the zoo, lumbered out of the storm. It fixed its black eyes on Zak before standing on its hind legs and stretching its mouth wide in a silent roar that revealed stained and terrible teeth.

Zak's chest tightened and his blood raced, and when the beast dropped on to all fours with a heavy thump, he tried to shout a warning to the others. But he couldn't speak. His voice caught in his throat as the bear lowered its head and started towards him, picking up speed. It thundered across the ice, an unstoppable monster. Zak stumbled backwards, closing his eyes and raising his arms in useless defence.

'You OK?' May's voice cut into his thoughts.

Zak was confused when no attack came. He opened his eyes.

'What are you doing, *freak*?'

He looked at his sister, and noticed the others had also stopped to watch him. 'You . . . you didn't see anything?'

May shook her head. 'You seeing polar bears again?'

'Umm . . .' Zak peered into the storm. 'No. No, course not. I just . . . I dunno, it must have been a gust of wind or something. You know. I slipped.'

May narrowed her eyes. 'You *sure* you're OK?'

'Yeah. Fine.' Zak thought he saw movement again, though. A dark shape moving away from the base. And there was a sound whispering in the wind. *Tick-tack-tick-*

tack. Tick-tack-tick-tack.

Like bear claws on the ice.

'What is it?' May followed Zak's gaze, and squinted at the swirling storm. Her face was lost inside the huge orange hood of her coat. She had made such a fuss about it in the shop – *Orange? I have to wear orange? Haven't they got a black one?* – but Mum said they both had to wear something 'high-vis' in Antarctica. Black wasn't an option.

'I guess I thought I saw something,' Zak said.

'You *are* seeing polar bears. What? They've flown down from the North Pole for a holiday, have they?'

'Oh, ha ha.' But when Zak turned to pull a face at her, he caught sight of the MRV and noticed something else out of place. Zak had seen enough photos to know what the vehicle was supposed to look like, and he could tell *something* was different about it. Something was missing.

He was afraid to say anything, though, in case he was imagining this too; in case his 'condition' was making him see things. But as he stared, a brief change in wind direction gave him a clear view, like windscreen wipers had swept across a foggy screen. It lasted no more than a fraction of a second, but Zak immediately knew what was wrong with the MRV. The place where Han and Chewie would sit when they were about to jump to light speed was gone. Instead of a blunted cockpit surrounded by windows, there was a ragged hole exposing the smashed-up interior of the vehicle.

Zak tried to understand what he was seeing. What could cause so much damage to such a strong vehicle? Then the storm changed, closing around the MRV once more, and he turned to May, wondering if he had even seen it at all.

'I saw it too.' Her eyes locked with his.

'We *all* saw it.' Mum came closer.

'Had to be the storm,' Dad said.

The storm? But it looked as if the MRV had been torn open. Or bitten. Like something big had grabbed that hunk of junk and bitten right through it the way Zak would bite the end off a chocolate bar. The wind couldn't do something like that, could it? Not even a giant polar bear could do *that.*

'Come on, we need to get inside,' Mum shouted against the wind.

Dad was the first to reach the stairs leading to The Hub. He grabbed the handrail and turned to check on the others. 'Everyone OK?' He put out a gloved thumbs-up.

One by one, they each replied with the same gesture, so Dad started up the steps, and the rest of them followed. When he reached the top, he slammed his fist on the door-control button.

Nothing happened.

'No power.' Dima shouted and pointed to a panel beside the door. 'Use the emergency.'

The panel was already half-open, so Dad stuck his fingers into the gap and pulled it the rest of the way. He dusted ice off the emergency lever, grabbed it, and yanked it downwards. It had frozen in place so it took a couple of attempts before there was a hollow *clunk*, a *hisssss*, and the door slid to one side, revealing the dark interior of The Hub.

'Come on.' Dad stood aside and ushered the others past him. 'Everybody in.'

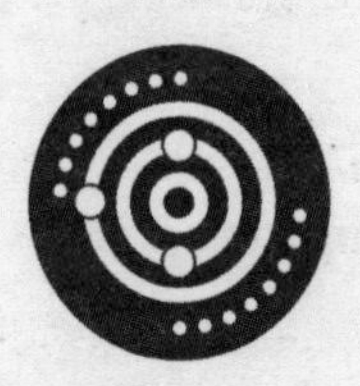

OUTPOST ZERO, ANTARCTICA
NOW

At home, Zak had this book called *It's A Strange World*. It was a heavy, bright green hardback with a fuzzy lenticular photo on the front – the kind that changes when you move it. From one angle, the picture was of a weird reptilian monster's head, green and leathery, with a huge mouth and small black eyes. But if you twisted it the other way, it turned into a human skull.

The book was full of photos and stories about the Unexplained. Bigfoot, the Tennessee Wildman, the Mothman, UFOs, stuff like that. One of Zak's favourite things was to sit in bed and study the pictures, trying to think of explanations for some of the weird things that happen in the world. One of the stories was about a ship called the *Mary Celeste* that was found drifting in the Atlantic Ocean. There was nothing wrong with the ship, and everyone's belongings were still on board, but the passengers and crew had disappeared. Gone.

Zak reckoned that when the sailors who found the *Mary Celeste* went on board, they must have felt the same way he did when he walked into The Hub. Everything about it was wrong. It was like stumbling into a spooky old graveyard at night.

When Dad closed the door, shutting out the howl of the wind, they stood in the darkness, no one saying anything. There wasn't enough light to see more than a few centimetres in front of them, and it was way colder than it should have been. There air was clammy and damp, and the smell was . . . Zak made himself breathe deeper, tasting the air . . . yeah, it was like a mixture of over-ripe fruit and raw meat. Like the greengrocer's and the butcher's at the end of a long, hot summer day.

And Zak wasn't the only one to notice it. He could tell *everyone* sensed something bad had happened here.

'Hello?' Dad's voice died as soon as it came out of his mouth. 'Anybody home?' There was no echo at all, as if something had snatched the sound away. 'Hello?'

Zak thought it was weird the way people did that, call 'hello' into the darkness. They always did it in films, as if the monster in the shadows was going to step out and wave with a smile. *Hello!*

'There are torches,' Dima said. There was a shuffle of boots followed by a patting sound. 'Here.' A click to Zak's left, and a bright beam pierced the darkness.

Dima shone the light at the wall beside the door, illuminating a rack with two torches still in it. Beside them, a red fire extinguisher hung from a bracket, and next to it was a chunky orange rifle that looked like the Nerf Elite Alpha Trooper Zak had at home.

Mum and Dad took a torch each. They switched them on and swept the beams around The Hub.

The room was a rectangle, with a door in each wall leading to different sections of the base. On the wall beside each door, there was a fire extinguisher and one of those orange rifles. In front of them, a spiral staircase corkscrewed up through the ceiling. To the right, red plastic chairs were pushed away from square tables. One chair lay on its back like someone had kicked it over in a struggle. There were paper napkin dispensers, plates glistening with congealed food, overturned mugs with their contents drying on the tabletops.

As the torch beams swept across the room, Zak caught sight of someone standing by the last table. He saw the figure for a fraction of a second but it was enough to notice the old-fashioned windproof clothes. It wore large fur mittens, with a bulky hood shrouding its head. A dark balaclava covered its face so no skin was visible, and goggles hid its eyes, giving it the appearance of a giant, bloated insect. It wasn't doing anything; just standing there. Watching them.

'What's that?' Zak grabbed Mum's hand and swept

the torch back.

Where the figure had been standing, the room was empty. But it had felt so *real*; exactly as Zak imagined Scott of the Antarctic would look.

'Is something there?' Mum asked. 'You see something?'

'No.' Zak let go of her hand and told himself to get a grip. 'Just a shadow.' This trip was going to be a nightmare if he jumped at every shadow in the dark. First the bear, and now this? They had been so real, though. What was *wrong* with him?

'We're going to be OK,' Mum said. 'You know that, right?'

'Yeah. Of course,' Zak said. 'I know.'

'Come on, we need to find out what happened here.' Dad ventured further into the room. 'Looks like they left in a hurry.'

'Left where, though?' May wondered. 'Where would they go? We're *literally* in the middle of nowhere.'

There was a pool table further over to the right; the balls and cues still out on the blue baize, casting long shadows as the torch beams passed over them. Close to it, an L-shaped sofa faced a screen on the back wall. There were deep impressions in the cushions where someone had been sitting.

'Ewww, what's that *smell*?' May said. 'It's like something died in here. Some holiday this is turning out to be.'

Zak stuck close to her. 'I thought you liked scary stuff.' He couldn't help glancing over at the place where he had seen the figure.

'Yeah, whatever. I like scary *films*, not *real* scary stuff.

Remind me why this place is called Outpost Zero. No, wait, I remember. It's because there's *zero* reason to come here.'

'Actually . . .' Zak imitated his dad by removing non-existent glasses, pinching the bridge of his nose, and deepening his voice. 'It's because Outpost *One* is being built on Mars. This base, right here, is what you might call Ground Zero for the Project.'

May snorted. Zak always did a pretty good impression of Dad.

'That's enough from you two,' Mum warned.

'Hello?' Dad called again as he led the group towards the spiral staircase.

'Hello!' Zak whispered in return. 'Who is it?'

May sniggered, but Dad ignored him.

'Is anyone there?' As Dad came closer to the stairs, something hard crunched under his boot and he stopped. 'What's that?' He aimed the light at his feet. 'Is that egg shells?'

'No, it's more like . . . I don't know.' Mum shone her torch at the floor and swept it around to illuminate more of the broken pieces. 'Insects?'

'Can't be.'

'No, you're right,' Zak said. 'They're like crushed insects. All dried up.' As the torchlight played over them, they shimmered in different colours.

'Nu-uh,' May said. 'There aren't any insects in Antarctica. Nothing but penguins, remember.'

'We'll find out soon enough.' Dad moved on towards the staircase.

On the first floor, one side of The Hub had a circular table with four computers on it. The other side was kitted out with a couple of treadmills, some weights, and gym equipment.

'Where is everyone?' May whispered. 'This is *proper* creepy.'

'No it isn't.' Mum spoke loudly, trying to break the atmosphere.

'Dr Reeves is right,' Dima agreed. 'Everything will be *horror show*.'

'What does that even mean?' May asked. 'You keep saying it, "horror show", and, honestly, it doesn't *sound* good.'

'Hmm? Oh, *khorosho*?' Dima chuckled. 'It is Russian. It means "fine". Everything is fine.'

'Yeah, well it doesn't sound like it,' May muttered.

'What we need is power,' Mum said. 'We need light and we need heat. It's already cold in here, and it's only going to get colder.

'I'll second that.' Dad raised his eyebrows at Dima, waiting for his agreement.

'*Da*. Sure.' Dima shrugged. 'We'll go and look at the generators, see if we–'

Screeeeee!

A screeching, tearing sound came from somewhere outside. Sudden and sharp, it broke through the quiet like a scream.

'Oh my God.' May was the first to speak. '*What . . .* was *that*?'

Screeeeee!

It was the shriek of metal being twisted and ripped apart. This time it went on for longer. Zak and May stared at each other, both of them with their eyes wide like they were going to pop right out of their heads.

'My plane!' Dima snapped into action, breaking away and sprinting for the stairs. His torch beam bobbed about, jittering through the darkness in a jerking, confusing flicker of light.

'Wait,' Dad called after him, but Dima was already thumping down the spiral staircase.

'Come on; stick together,' Dad said, but before they had taken more than a few steps, they heard a sharp yelp followed by a series of bumps.

When they found Dima, he was lying on his back at the bottom of the stairs, not moving. His torch had rolled under the table and was shining across the floor in a cone of white light that illuminated him on one side, and threw his shadow across The Hub on the other.

Mum and Dad went straight to him, but May and Zak stayed at the bottom of the staircase, staring.

'Is he dead?' Zak wondered.

'Of course not,' said May. 'He can't be. Can he?'

Mum checked Dima over while Dad shone his torch at him. The pilot's face was a mask of blood. It was everywhere. Running down his coat, on his hood, on the floor . . . *everywhere.*

'Where's it all coming from?' Dad's breath was like mist

in the torchlight.

'I don't know. I can't see a thing.' Mum held out her torch. 'May, get some paper napkins from the table.'

May hesitated.

'*Quickly!*'

She grabbed Mum's torch and ran across The Hub, snatching up one of the napkin dispensers. When she returned, Mum pulled out a handful and patted them on Dima's face to soak up the blood. The napkins were drenched through in seconds, and Mum dropped them on to the floor with a disgusting wet *splotch* that made Zak's stomach heave.

She grabbed another handful. 'Shine the torch here,' she said to Dad and May, who stood over her like lampposts. 'And here . . .' She worked her way around Dima's face until she found the large gash on his forehead, then she wadded a pile of napkins together and pressed them hard against the wound.

As she did it, Dima opened his eyes and blinked in confusion. '*Moy samolyet*,' he mumbled, before closing his eyes again.

'A wound like that needs stitches,' Dad said. 'Or glue, or something. We need a first aid kit.'

'What we need,' Mum said, 'is some power. I can't see a thing and it's getting colder by the minute. If we don't get the generators working, this wound won't matter; we'll all free–'

'Evelyn.' Dad cut her short but Zak knew what she had been about to say. *We'll all freeze to death*. That was the truth of it. It was minus forty degrees outside, and getting colder inside by the minute. They needed heat and light or they were going to die.

Zak stared at Dima, caught in the torch beams like he was under lights on an operating table. Beside him, Mum's hands were covered in blood as if she was in the middle of some kind of crazy surgery. The sight of it made him sick. It made him think of mad doctors *(Zak Reeves? Ah yes, it's time for your operation. Come along, this won't hurt a bit . . .)* and sinister hospitals, and the awful thing growing inside his head. It made him think of the electric bone saw he'd seen on TV when he'd walked in on May watching *Re-Animator* with her friends. It made him think of pain and dying.

And as all those things tumbled through his mind, an ache began behind his right eye, and pulsed across the top of his head.

The ache squeezed and relaxed, squeezed and relaxed, growing more intense. Zak put a hand to the side of his head, where a scar was barely visible beneath his short, dark hair. He traced a finger along the ridge of scarred skin, then a sudden, intense pain seared through his mind. In an instant, the world fell away into nothing. He was hanging in the air over an infinite black sea, its surface shimmering like an oil slick. His ears were filled with the clicking and rustling of endless movement.

This isn't happening. Zak squeezed his eyes shut. *This isn't happening.* He shook his head and opened his eyes to see he was back in The Hub. Mum and Dad were there,

Dima was on the floor, and May was standing close by.

But they weren't alone.

The figure was back. The explorer. It stood beyond the reach of the torchlight, head shrouded, face hidden, eyes covered by those creepy goggles. As Zak watched, the figure raised its right hand and extended it towards him. Its mouth moved beneath the balaclava, and in that moment, Zak was certain the shrouded figure was Death.

Not now, Zak thought. *It can't end here. Not like this. I'm not ready. We need lights and warmth and for everybody to be OK because it's just supposed to be me and–*

And in a blink the figure was gone. It didn't fade; it disappeared as if it had never been there. The pain in his head switched off, and there was a flicker of light from the ceiling.

Once.

Twice.

Then, in a blaze of light and a blast of warmth, the power came back on across Outpost Zero.

JANUARY ISLAND, SOUTH CHINA SEA
17 HOURS AGO

The Broker sipped his drink and stared out at the trail of reflected sun blazing across the sea beyond the balcony. Ice clinked in his glass, condensation dripped around his fingers, and the cold water soothed his throat. As he took in the view, he ran through the events that had happened in Costa Rica last week, but his thoughts were brought into focus when a large-screened smartphone lit up on the table beside his wicker chair.

It displayed the word '**Phoenix**', and began to ring.

The Broker let the phone ring three times before leaning forward to place his glass on the coaster beside it. He was careful to line up the bottom of the glass exactly with the circular pattern on the coaster. When it was done, he dried his fingers on a crisp white napkin and touched the green button.

He leant back in his chair and closed his eyes, saying nothing.

'Sir, I have something for you,' said the woman at the other end of the call.

'Go on.' The Broker's voice was deep and pleasant. His tone was neutral and there was no trace of an accent.

'One of your operatives at NASA contacted me with something a few minutes ago. I've prepared a package.'

'Send it.'

With a gentle *ping*, an icon popped up in the top right-hand corner of The Broker's smartphone. He opened his eyes and leant forward to touch it. Straight away, an image opened on the screen. 'Tell me what I'm looking at.'

'Less than an hour ago, a satellite passed over Antarctica and took a series of photographs. The man at NASA who is assigned to monitoring the satellite is one of your operatives, sir, and he called me straight away. He thought you should see the photographs. This is exactly the kind of information that matches your particular interests. And it's linked to BioMesa, sir, which is high on your watch list.'

The Broker said nothing. This new information was interesting, but he didn't want to hope for too much. When he was ready, he reached for the smartphone and picked it up. The image was mostly white, with stormy swirls like an abstract painting. Hidden in the spiralling patterns, though, were the dark shapes of buildings formed into a T-Shape. The Broker could also make out the faint markings of a landing strip and one or two outbuildings.

On the other end of the line, Phoenix watched a mirror image of what her employer was seeing. 'Apologies for the image quality, sir, they're currently experiencing adverse weather conditions over Antarctica, but you're looking at Outpost Zero. As you know, it's a training facility for–'

'Don't tell me what I already know.'

'Of course, sir. Please forgive–'

'Get on with it.'

'In the second image, sir, you'll see an object in the centre of the landing strip.'

The Broker flicked to the next image and, sure enough, there was a large oval object visible through the storm.

'We believe that to be one of the Spiders, sir. You've seen the blueprints.'

'Yes, I know I have.' The Broker admired the ingenuity Drs Evelyn and Adam Reeves had shown in the construction of the Spider drones. He had even considered taking control of the project for himself. The drones would fetch a high price. But he had become more interested in what BioMesa was doing in Antarctica. BioMesa had sent a group of researchers to Outpost Zero, and The Broker suspected they were breaking regulations, searching for something beneath the ice. Oil, perhaps. Gas, or some other resource he wasn't yet aware of. Whatever it was, he wanted to know about it. 'I hope this is good, Phoenix. I'm afraid you have caught me in a rather dour mood.'

'I'll get to the point, sir.'

'I wish you would.'

'If you flip through the images, sir, you'll notice the Spider drones have been rather active. And there's evidence to suggest they have been building things beyond their usual instructions. It's as if the drones are acting alone.'

'Alone?' The Broker leant forward. 'Are you suggesting some kind of artificial Intelligence?'

'Your man at NASA doesn't think so. He suspects something else. You'll see that he's used thermal imaging to enhance the last few pictures, sir, and . . .'

The Broker stopped listening. What he saw in those last few photographs made him stand and walk to the edge of the balcony. He closed his eyes and took a deep breath of fresh air. When he had filled his lungs and calmed his mind, he switched his focus back to the last three pictures displayed on the device he was holding.

Each image showed him a grey land of ice and snow. In the first, though, the buildings of Outpost Zero were a dull orange, emitting a heat signature lower than he would have expected. There were three red blobs on the landing strip, and he guessed they must be the Spiders – the drones. The blobs were about the right size and shape. In the second image, the buildings had lost heat and were now only a faint orange. The Spiders had moved to the front of the base, but without good video footage it was impossible to tell exactly what they were doing. None of those things concerned him, though. There was something else far more important about the image.

About a kilometre east of Outpost Zero, there was now a large, bright orange patch. The Broker flicked between the two images again, seeing how the patch appeared as if from nowhere.

He glanced at the time coding on the pictures and saw they were taken sixty minutes apart. In the short space of an hour, something had appeared beneath the ice. Something warm.

The Broker flicked to the third, most recent, image and paused to process what he was seeing. 'Do we know how deep that is?'

'It's impossible to tell without being on the ground, sir.'

'And how soon *can* we have men on the ground?' The Broker knew Phoenix would have an answer. That's why he paid her so well – because she was smart and efficient.

'We have the two prototype Ospreys you acquired, sir. I know they're to be sold to your buyers in Russia, but they're currently at November Island, so I have taken the liberty of ordering them to be fuelled and waiting on the tarmac. Analysis suggests they're the best-suited aircraft for this operation. I've contacted Lazarovich, and instructed her to assemble her team. They will arrive at November Island with all the necessary equipment within the next ten hours. The Ospreys don't have the range, but the pilots assure me they can refuel mid-air and be on site in eleven hours. We can have our teams at Outpost Zero in just over twenty hours, sir.'

The Broker raised his eyes to the view beyond the balcony and watched the waves cresting. 'Good. Make sure Lazarovich gets everything she needs. Does anybody else know about this?'

'No, sir.'

'You're sure?'

'One hundred per cent, sir.'

'Keep it that way. Make sure my man at NASA buries those images. And I want someone working on all communications coming in and out of Outpost Zero. Take complete control of it. The base needs to be sealed tight.'

'About that, sir . . .'

'Why do I have the feeling you are about to disappoint me, Phoenix?'

'I'm afraid we have been unable to take control of communications at the base, sir. It seems somebody else has already done that.'

'Who?'

'We don't know. Everything has been shut down from inside Outpost Zero. The only thing working is a primitive email system, and even that is only intermittent. Something is happening out there, sir, but we're not quite sure what.'

'All right. Keep on those communications; I want to know everything that happens.' The Broker cut off the call but stayed where he was on the balcony, watching the sea. It was particularly calm today. He paused to take in the view and settle his thoughts before once again studying the image on his tablet.

The snow, the base, the Spiders. And something else.

The second thermal image had shown the appearance of something warm beneath the ice. The third image showed how much it had grown; like a wide, orange river running towards Outpost Zero. Something was buried deep in the ice and it was either warming up, or it was growing. Whatever it was, The Broker was certain it was the reason why BioMesa was in Antarctica. They were searching for something. They had *found* something. And, as far as he was concerned, it now belonged to him.

Perhaps this wasn't going to be such a bad day after all.

OUTPOST ZERO, ANTARCTICA
NOW

Under the glare of the overhead spotlights, Dima sat at one of the tables pressing a wad of napkins to his forehead. Dad rummaged through a first aid kit, but it was obvious he didn't have a clue what he was doing, and was just trying to look busy. Mum had gone to the Medical Station in the East Tunnel – she said it was better to bring what she needed rather than try to move Dima in this state.

Zak was squatting close to the bottom of the spiral staircase, with his back to the bloodstain on the floor. He was studying the broken pieces of shell that had crunched under their boots earlier.

'What do they look like to you?' he said to May who was sitting on the stairs.

'I dunno.'

'They look like beetle wings.'

'I already told you; there's no beetles in Antarctica.'

The shards were as black as death but when he turned his head Zak could see hints of red and green and blue. 'There's loads of them. They're everywhere.' He gestured at the broken pieces scattered around The Hub.

'Got to be something else,' May said.

'Like what? What do *you* think they are, Dad?'

'We'll ask the Project members when we find them.' Dad continued to sort through the first aid kit. 'What's taking your mum so long? What's she–'

The door to the East Tunnel hissed and Mum came back into The Hub. She went straight to where Dima was sitting and opened the small box she'd brought with her. 'This'll do the trick.' She took out a gadget that looked like a chef's blowtorch, and fiddled with a couple of dials on the side of it. Dima moaned when she moved his hand away from the cut and wiped it clean before switching on the instrument. A dull red glow appeared at its tip.

'What's that?' May went over to watch.

'This, my darling, is a very sophisticated Dermal Adhesion Unit.'

'Which is?'

'Basically, it's a glue gun. It seals the wound.'

'Oh.' May leant closer, watching how Mum pinched Dima's cut together with one hand and touched the tip of the instrument against it. 'You mean it heals him?'

'In a manner of speaking.'

'Cool.' Zak risked a peek despite feeling squeamish at the sight of all the gore. 'How does it work?'

'Haven't a clue; I just know it does.' Mum didn't take her eyes off what she was doing.

'It's awesome.' Zak watched as Dima's skin glued back together. 'But also kind of disgusting.'

As the wound grew smaller, a large glob of blood welled up and plopped out, running down Dima's forehead. Zak turned away. 'Gross.'

'Wimp.' May smiled.

'No I'm not.'

'Yes you are. Can't stand a bit of blood?'

'Well, it *is* pretty rank.'

'Why don't you two go and sit over there?' Dad suggested, and Zak was pleased for the excuse to walk away.

'I want to watch,' May complained.

'I think it's best if you two stick together,' Mum said.

Reluctantly, May joined Zak and they perched themselves on the edge of the L-shaped sofa, neither of them settling back into the impressions left by the previous occupants. It would have been too much like lying in someone else's bed. Or grave.

'Don't you think it's freaky?' May said.

'The skin thing? Totally. It's disgusting.'

'That's not what I meant. I meant the way everything came back on? I mean, it's like someone knew we needed the power. When you think about it, the same thing happened when we were trying to land. *Literally* the same thing.' May had taken off her gloves and was picking at the nail polish on one finger. 'If they hadn't come on, we'd have crashed. It's like they came back on exactly when we needed them. Both times.' She broke off a small black flake. 'That's weird, right?'

'Yeah. Like everything else in this place.' He stood and paced backwards and forwards a couple of times before heading to the window. Flurries still twisted and swirled out there, but the worst of the storm had died down and visibility was better than before. The landing strip beacons shone into the mist like giant yellow lightsabers. Zak counted fifteen lights on each side of the runway, and between the twelfth, Dima's plane sat on the compacted ice, tilted forward as if it had lost its balance.

Zak put his face closer to the window and cupped his hands to block out the reflection from inside The Hub. He squinted at the plane, trying to make sense of what he was seeing. The front skid of the aircraft was missing, that's why it was tilted forward, but that wasn't the only thing wrong with it. Similar to the MRV, it looked as if someone had taken a massive bite out of it. The cockpit was torn open and a large, jagged piece of metal the size of a garage door lay on the runway. Beside it were the pilot's and co-pilot's seats, torn from their fixings and tossed aside like someone had dumped some old rubbish.

Digging his phone from his pocket, Zak switched on the camera, held it against the window and zoomed in as far as it would go. He focused on the cockpit of the plane. The picture was fuzzy but it was obvious all the instruments were gone. All those switches Dima had flicked, all those controls he had used, all those warnings that had flashed on and off, were gone. Not broken or smashed-up; *gone*.

'My God, what happened?' May startled him.

'I . . . don't know,' he said. 'But it's not going to fly us out of here.'

'Mum? Dad? You'd better come and see this.'

'What is it, May, we're busy?' Mum was inspecting Dima's wound, checking it would stay sealed.

'Seriously, you want to see this.'

Dad's expression darkened. 'See what?'

'The plane,' Zak said. 'It's the same as the MRV; like something took a bite out of it.'

'Don't be ridiculous.' Dad came over. 'You'd better not be–' He stopped in his tracks when he saw it. 'Oh my God.' Then Mum was coming over to see, and even Dima managed to shuffle over to the window.

They stood in a line, gaping at what was left of the aircraft.

'Moy samolyet,' Dima whispered. 'My plane. This is not *khorosho.* Not at all.'

Dad took off his glasses and rubbed his eyes with the back of his hand before looking again. 'What could have done that?'

'Well, I'm pretty sure it wasn't penguins.' Dima managed just one sentence before his knees buckled and he crumpled to the floor.

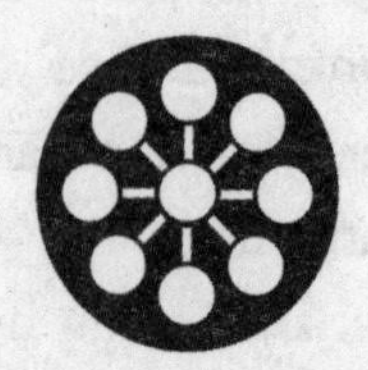

OUTPOST ZERO, ANTARCTICA
NOW

Dad helped Dima to the L-shaped sofa by the pool table, while Mum nagged him, saying he shouldn't be moving about. 'You've probably got concussion,' she said. 'And you've lost a lot of blood. You need to sit down and *stay* sitting down.'

When she mentioned blood, Zak looked over at the patch of it drying on the floor at the bottom of the staircase. There were drips and splashes where Dima had been lying. And the bloody paper towels were gross. The place was like a crime scene.

'Zak? May? Why don't you two see if you can find Dima

something to eat?' Mum pointed to the kitchen at the far side of the Hub. 'And bring some water.'

Zak could tell Mum and Dad wanted them out of the way, and as soon as they went to the kitchen he heard Dad say, 'What the hell is going on here?' He had never been much good at whispering. 'Where is everyone? And the plane? I don't want to frighten the kids, but this isn't good.'

'I think they're already frightened.'

'We shouldn't have brought them here. Especially Zak. What were we thinking? What if something happens to him?'

Oh no, this again. Poor old Zak.

'We weren't to know it would be like this,' Mum said. 'We expected experts, state of the art medical facilities, clinical conditions and–'

'We should have sent them back to stay with my sister.'

'Well, it's too late to be blaming ourselves,' Mum said. '*And* it's a waste of time. We can worry about all that later. What we need to do now is figure out how to put this right.'

Dad sighed. 'Do you think it might be something to do with–'

Whoosh! Zak didn't hear the rest because May turned on the tap and water jetted out at top speed. It hammered into the metal sink and sprayed everywhere.

'Shh!' he snapped at her.

'What?' She turned it down and grabbed a glass from the draining board.

'I'm trying to listen.' Zak tilted his head, peering over in Mum and Dad's direction. *Something to do with what?* he was wondering, but he'd missed it now.

'I know,' Dad was saying, 'but what else could have done that? Out here?'

'You're jumping to conclusions. We'd have to get a good look at the damage. And we need to see if they're still . . .' Mum glanced over and saw Zak watching them. She forced a smile at him, and leant closer to Dad. When she spoke again, she lowered her voice so Zak couldn't hear.

'What do you think that's all about?' Zak asked May.

'Who knows?' She filled the glass. 'I think they're trying not to scare us. You know what they're like; they think we can't handle anything, but they have *no* idea. God, imagine if they had to put up with Vanessa Morton-Chandler and her clones every day. They wouldn't last five minutes at school. *Literally*.' She sounded tough, but her hand was trembling as she put the glass on the worktop and wiped it dry with a towel.

Zak was thinking about the figure again. The explorer he'd seen (*imagined?*) earlier in The Hub when the lights were out. He wanted to tell May about it, as if getting it out in the open would make it less horrible. She'd think he was mad, of course, probably make fun of him like she usually did – call him a freak and stuff – but the urge to say something was too strong to resist. So he tried to think of a way to tell her, without actually telling her.

'I read this story online,' he said, leaning both hands on the kitchen worktop. 'About some . . . researcher guy from one of these small bases out here. They were investigating meteors, right out in the middle of nowhere. Apparently there's meteors hitting this place all the time. The Antarctic, that is, not this exact place right here.'

'Yeah, I realized.'

'OK. Well. Anyway, the story is: one of the researchers went out on his snowmobile to find a meteor, but there was a storm and he got lost. He found an old abandoned shack instead, like a cabin that explorers or researchers used in the past. I saw a photo – there was still food and supplies in there, like really old tins that were rusted and falling apart. Apparently there are loads of these things all over the place – ships, bases, I even saw a photo of an old church sitting out on the ice in the middle of nowhere, and–'

'Is there a point to this, or are you trying to make me feel even worse about this place?'

'Umm.' Zak hesitated. Maybe this wasn't a good idea.

May sighed and opened a cupboard. 'Just tell me the rest of the story.'

'OK. So, this guy, he went into the old shack, and the minute he stepped inside, he knew something was wrong.'

'Hm,' May said. 'Like when we came in here.'

'Yeah, I suppose. Except, he felt like people had *died* in there–'

'I know *that* feeling.'

'– like maybe a part of them was left behind like a ghost or something. But he was cold and hungry and the storm was getting worse, so he stayed. There was a bed and stuff, so he went to sleep, but he woke up, and there were people standing around him. At first he thought they were there to rescue him, but he realized they weren't wearing ECW gear like they should have been, not like this stuff . . .' Zak pinched the front of his thick orange coat to show May what he meant. 'These guys were wearing old-timey cold weather gear. Like *really* old-fashioned.'

'Don't tell me; they killed him?'

'No. They just stood there staring at him, then they turned around and left the shack. He was scared, like pee-your-pants scared, and stayed where he was, didn't leave the shack until he plucked up the courage to go outside, but there was no one there. And when the storm cleared and he went back to base, he took some people out to investigate, but they couldn't find the shack. It's like it was never there.'

'So how did they get the photo?'

'Hm?'

'Of the shack. You said you saw a photo.'

'I dunno.' Zak shook his head. 'I suppose they used a photo of a different shack for the article. Does it matter?'

May stood there with one hand on the open cupboard door, her head turned towards Zak. 'You saying you think there are ghosts out here?'

'No.' Zak wanted to tell her what he had seen, but he didn't want her to think it was his illness making him see things. He had to know what she thought of the story.

May sighed. 'He was hungry and exhausted, right?'

'I suppose.'

'So he must have been seeing things.' She turned back to the cupboard. 'It can happen. People hallucinate when they're tired and hungry. Or sick. I like horror films, Zak, but I don't believe in ghosts.'

When she said that, Zak knew he couldn't tell her what he'd seen; May was scared enough already. She would blame it on his illness, and maybe she'd be right. Maybe he *had* imagined it.

'C'mon,' May said. 'Let's get something for Dima to eat.'

The kitchen was well stocked. There were cupboards full of baked beans and canned vegetables, tea, coffee, dried milk, and piles of vacuum-packed foil bags with things like 'Beef Stew' and 'Chicken Curry' printed on them.

'Astronaut ice cream?' May held up a foil pack.

'Why? What's the point? This place is basically a giant freezer, they could have as much proper ice cream as they wanted.'

'Yeah, 'cause all they have to do is milk all the Antarctic cows they have around the base.'

'Or they could fly it in like they do with all this other stuff.' Zak tore the lid off a large plastic container full of chocolate bars and showed it to May. 'Isn't sugar supposed to be good for you if you've had a shock?'

'Yep.' She grabbed a Snickers and they went back to where the others were waiting. Zak pocketed one of the chocolate bars for later, and followed her.

'So, what's the plan now?' May handed the water and the Snickers to Dima.

'Well.' Dad sat down. 'Now we have power, there are two main priorities – find the Project members, and get a message out to Head Office. We need to let them know what's going on.'

'Do we even *know* what's going on?' May said.

'No,' Dima mumbled as he took a bite of the Snickers. 'But it doesn't look good.'

'Well, let's see shall we?' Mum glared at him. 'We've got power, so comms should be fine, and that means we'll be able to get someone here in a few hours. That's no time at all, right?'

'Right.' Dad stood and headed towards The Hub entrance, where a rough map was stuck to the wall by the door. The map was home-made, as if someone had been at a loose end and decided to do a bit of doodling. It was held in place by a small piece of duct tape.

Dad tapped the image of the Control module, the first building off the East Tunnel, and looked back at Mum. 'You work on communications; you're better with that stuff than I am.'

'Nice to hear you admit it,' Mum said.

'You've already been in Medical, but check it again. And make sure you check the Science building – see if you can find anyone. I'll take the West and North Tunnels, and when we're done, we'll meet back in Control.' He tapped the map again. 'They have to be here somewhere.'

'OK, you come with me.' Mum touched May's shoulder. 'Zak, you stay here with Dima while Dad checks the–'

'No way. I'm not staying here. I'll go with Dad.'

'Is that a good idea?' Mum asked. 'Do you feel OK?'

'*Yes*. Why do I have to keep telling you? I'm fine, Mum. No one ever listens.'

Mum paused. 'OK. You go with Dad.' She turned towards the East Tunnel. 'May and I will go this way.'

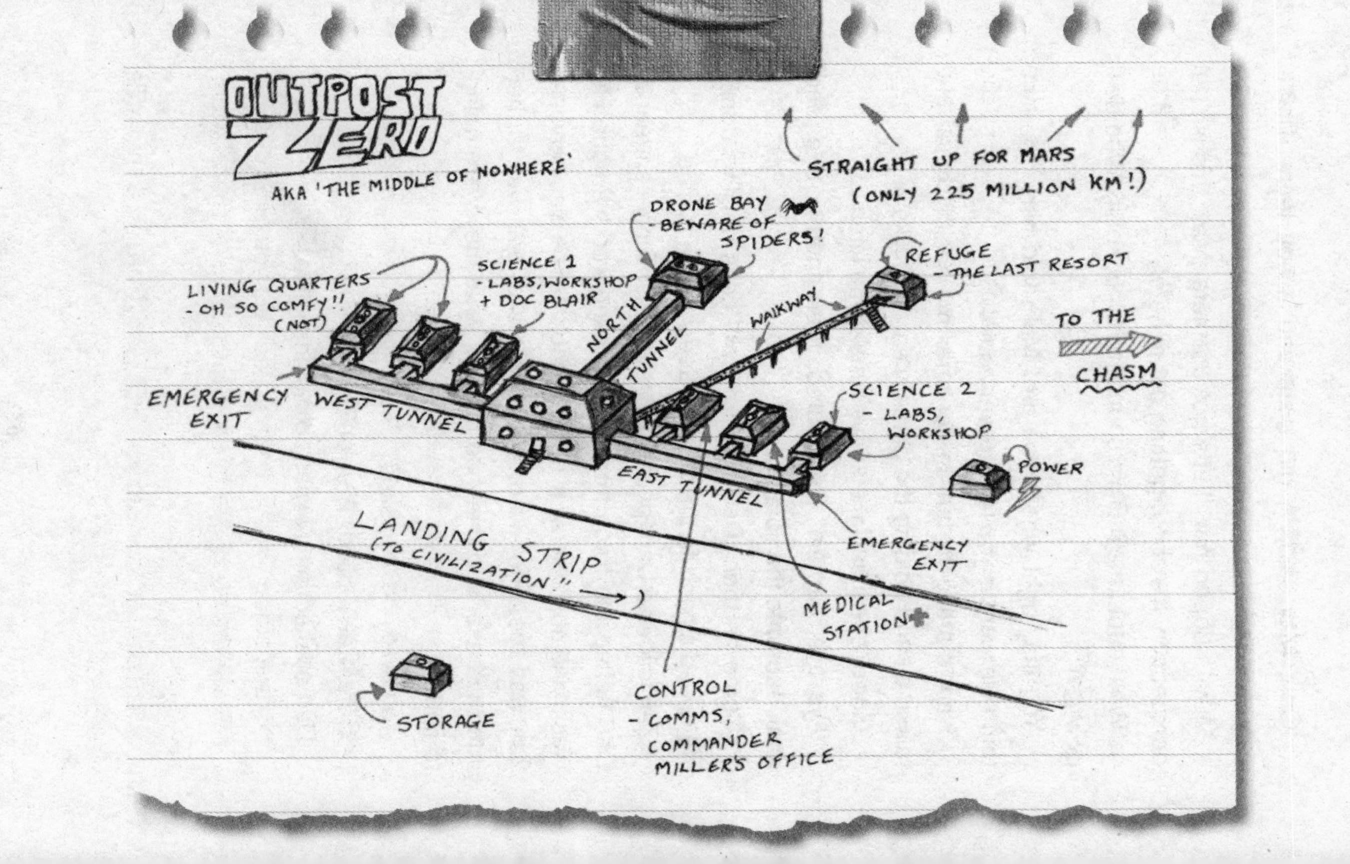
OUTPOST ZERO
AKA 'THE MIDDLE OF NOWHERE'
STRAIGHT UP FOR MARS
(ONLY 225 MILLION KM!)
DRONE BAY
- BEWARE OF SPIDERS!
REFUGE
- THE LAST RESORT
LIVING QUARTERS
- OH SO COMFY!! (NOT)
SCIENCE 1
- LABS, WORKSHOP + DOC BLAIR
NORTH TUNNEL
WALKWAY
TO THE CHASM
EMERGENCY EXIT
WEST TUNNEL
SCIENCE 2
- LABS, WORKSHOP
POWER
EAST TUNNEL
LANDING STRIP
(TO CIVILIZATION!!)
EMERGENCY EXIT
MEDICAL STATION
STORAGE
CONTROL
- COMMS, COMMANDER MILLER'S OFFICE

'Ooh,' May said. 'A girl team and a boy team. That's very modern.'

Mum stopped her. 'Let's not go there, May, this isn't a competition. It's about getting out of here.'

'What about me?' Dima sounded half out of it. 'Who do I go with?'

'You stay right where you are,' Mum told him. 'The last thing we want is you falling over again.'

'I am starting to feel better after my healthy meal.' He raised a hand holding the partially eaten Snickers.

'Good, because I'm sure we'll need you later.'

'Aye aye, captain.' He saluted, took another bite, and sank back into the sofa.

'Come on then.' Dad nudged Zak. 'Let's get this done.' He raised a hand to the others. 'See you in a minute.'

Zak followed Dad, pausing by the West Tunnel entrance. Dad hefted the torch from his left hand into his right. He was trying not to show it, but Zak could tell he was nervous. Zak was too. They were about to make their way further into the base, and they had no idea what they were going to find.

'You ready?' Dad asked.

'Sure,' Zak replied. 'Are you?'

Dad pushed his glasses up his nose. 'No.'

OUTPOST ZERO, ANTARCTICA
NOW

The West Tunnel was a long, windowless corridor with pale blue walls and a pale blue floor. White light flooded from spots embedded in the ceiling, giving it a clinical atmosphere.

The dull ached prodded behind Zak's right eye again. It nudged him, reminding him of hospitals and how much more time he would have to spend in them. He checked Dad wasn't watching, and pressed the palm of his hand against his eye, waggling it about, trying to get rid of the ache.

'You OK, dude?' Dad stopped.

Dude? Zak cringed. It was so awkward when Dad tried

to be cool. Dad was tall and lean with the beginning of 'middle-aged spread' as he called it – or a 'pot belly' as Mum called it. He had short silver hair that was thinning on top, and was partial to brown corduroy trousers and brown shoes. He sometimes wore a jacket with elbow patches – like Zak's geography teacher – and in the summer, he was even known to wear socks and sandals. Zak loved his dad, but he didn't believe he had ever been cool.

'Everything OK?' Dad asked again.

'Yeah.' Zak blinked hard. 'Don't *you* start.'

'OK . . .' Dad watched him. 'It's just that you seemed a bit spooked when we arrived. And I guess the blood made you queasy, so I was wondering if–'

'I'm fine, Dad.'

Fine, fine, fine. Zak was sick of telling people he was fine. Why did they never listen?

'All right. Well . . . I guess we'll check the sleeping quarters first,' Dad said. 'Maybe they're all taking a well-earned nap.'

At the far end of the tunnel, Dad stood with his hand hovering over the door-control button, and grinned at Zak as if he was ashamed for being nervous. He pressed it, and when the door to the living quarters hissed open, he raised the torch like he was expecting trouble.

But the short corridor beyond was empty. Dad let out his breath and switched on a light that flickered once, twice, then illuminated a central aisle with three large, round windows in the ceiling. In the summer months, light would flood through those windows, but for now Antarctica was in darkness twenty-four hours a day.

On either side of the corridor, five doors gave access to the separate quarters. They were all open.

'Hello?' Dad's voice wavered slightly.

No one replied.

Of course *no one replied. There's no one here.*

Entering the corridor, Zak noticed more of the broken shards glistening on the floor. 'Just like in The Hub,' he whispered.

Dad considered the fragments before turning to the first door on his left. 'Let's see if anyone's here.'

The small, basic living quarters were made up of a tiny sitting room, a bathroom that wasn't much bigger than the kind Zak had seen on aeroplanes, and two narrow bedrooms with bunk beds and built-in wardrobes. There was a handful of paperbacks on the shelf in the sitting room, and a few photos in frames on the wall. In one photo, a family of four stood on a snowy mountainside, wearing skis and smiling for the camera. In another, two of them – Mum and daughter, Zak guessed from the likeness – were posing in front of Outpost Zero, where the sky was bright blue in contrast to the whiteness of the ice. Other photos showed the son holding some kind of certificate in front of him, and the daughter, about the same age as May, dressed in a school jumper.

In one of the bedrooms, there was a single piece of white paper stuck to the wall. In simple black lettering it said 'Be Prepared' and right below that were the words 'Improvise, adapt and overcome.'

'Come on,' Dad said. 'This place is empty, let's check the others.'

So Zak took one last glance and followed Dad along the corridor checking the rest of the living quarters. Each one was identical in design, and each one was brightened up with a few personal items. In the last room, however, the contents of the shelves were scattered on the floor, and the chairs were overturned. Tiny black fragments lay everywhere among the personal belongings.

'What happened in *here*?' Zak said. 'Looks like there was a fight or something.'

Dad raised his eyebrows and shook his head. When he turned to Zak, he smiled and said, 'Nobody home, I guess. Let's check the–'

'I know what you're doing. Pretending you're not worried. Pretending everything's OK.'

'Everything *is* OK,' Dad said. 'We'll get to the bottom of this. You let me and Mum worry about it. It's not your job to worry about things like this.'

Zak glanced round the last room again, his gaze coming to rest on a bobble head figure of Star-Lord from *Guardians of the Galaxy* lying on the floor among all those weird black fragments. 'So where do you think they are?'

'Well, they have to be somewhere. People don't just disappear.'

'And what about the MRV? And the plane? How did that happen?'

Dad shook his head. 'The storm, I guess.'

'The *storm*? No way. The wind couldn't do that.'

'So what do *you* think it was?'

Zak thought about polar bears that shouldn't be there, and ghostly explorers, but he shook his head and said, 'I don't know.'

'Exactly.' Dad moved back into the tunnel. 'So let's see if we can find out what's going on.'

But the second living area was as empty as the first, and Zak found himself hoping Mum and May had more luck. There was only the lab left for them to search on this side of the base, and every empty room they went into had him more and more certain something terrible had happened at Outpost Zero.

In the lab, Zak recognized some of the kit as better versions of the apparatus they had at school – Bunsen burners, beakers, tripods, microscopes – but the rest of it was stuff he'd never seen before. He had no idea what most of it was, but right at the back of the main room there were two sealed labs, and one them contained a large machine similar to the MRI scanner they used at the hospital to check out the inside of his head.

On every wall, there was a fire extinguisher; right next to more of those orange Nerf gun things he'd seen in The Hub. Zak put his hand on the one beside the door, wondering what it was for.

'That's an RCDS,' Dad said. 'Ranged Chemical Delivery System. Catchy name, isn't it?'

'Yeah, totally. Not.'

Dad smiled. 'That's scientists for you. Invent something

awesome and give it a rubbish name.'

'You mean like "Spider Drones"?'

'You don't think it's a good name for them?'

'Dad, no one likes spiders.'

'Maybe.' He pointed at the RCDS. 'Anyway, it's a kind of rifle. Fire's a big concern here, and it will be when they get to Mars – you can't just call the fire brigade, right? So BioMesa came up with this idea to help out. It uses compressed air to fire small canisters that burst on contact. They're filled with chemicals that extinguish the fire. Not much good for a big fire, but for something small, it's perfect. We call it a Ranger for short.' Dad turned to leave. 'We'll have a go later, how about that?'

'OK.' But as Zak was about to follow Dad back into the tunnel, he saw something that made him stop.

'What's wrong?' Dad asked.

Zak ignored him and headed deeper into the room. He went to a bench by the far-left wall. 'You need to see this.'

There were three bugs, each roughly the length of his little finger, lying on a white dissection board. One of the bugs was on its front. Its body was cone-shaped, and segmented as if it were wearing armour. It had a round head at the wider end, and something like a pincer at its tail end. To Zak, it looked like a cross between a scorpion and an earwig. Its armour plating was black, but when Zak tilted his head, he saw flickers of colour, like when a sheen of petrol shimmers on the surface of a puddle.

'It's like all those little bits we found everywhere,' he whispered.

The segment immediately below the bug's head was marked with two faint yellow circles. Wings, two on each side, were splayed out from beneath the armour plating, as if someone had pulled them out to display them.

Beside it was a similar bug, lying on its back. Someone had cut this one down the middle and removed whatever was inside the shell. Next to it, there was a fleshy, grey, caterpillar-like bug – except it wasn't a caterpillar because it had six pairs of short legs.

'What is it?' Zak said. 'Some kind of insect?'

Dad puffed his cheeks and blew out. 'I don't know much about insects, but I'm pretty sure they only have three sets of legs.' He found a tablet computer lying beside the dissection board and switched it on. It lit up immediately, showing a document which had the words 'Core Sample #31' written at the top, followed by a long list of numbers and charts and tables.

Zak watched as Dad scrolled through it, his frown growing deeper and deeper.

'What does it say?'

Dad tapped the screen. 'I'm not sure. It looks like a lot of DNA information. Something about genomes and stem cells and–' His attention switched from the tablet computer to the creatures on the board, to the tablet again. '– and a list of species.'

'Species?'

'Mmm. Mammals, reptiles, birds, fish . . . insects . . . everything, basically. I don't understand, though, because according to this, all this information has come from Ice

Core Thirty-One.'

'Why is that weird?'

'Well, firstly, no one here has been taking ice core samples – at least not as far as I know – and secondly, it's impossible to have found all this DNA in one sample. You'd have to scour the planet to gather this kind of information. Take DNA from every animal you could find. It doesn't make sense.'

Zak inspected the insects, or whatever they were, and shivered. 'They give me the creeps.'

'They're even worse when they're alive,' Dad said.

'*What?*'

'These ones are alive. Come and look.' Dad was heading towards a tall glass container at the far end of the long bench.

Zak wasn't sure he wanted to see them, but they were behind glass. What harm could they do?

The glass container was like a tall fish tank, about two metres high and a metre wide. From where he was standing, Zak could see some of the black bugs, motionless at the bottom. As he went closer, the bugs began to move. Some crawled to the front, butting against the glass, and others spread their wings from beneath their armour and fluttered upwards to clatter against the top of the container.

'There's quite a few of them in here,' Dad said. 'I wonder where they came from.'

Inside the tank, the bugs grew more and more agitated, all of them now spreading their wings and scattering around the container in a swirl. Their armour battered against the glass, *ting-ting-ting*, in a bizarre rhythm. They moved faster and faster, becoming a blur of black that shimmered with hints of colour. And, right in the centre of the swirling swarm, two bright yellow streaks appeared. Zak had seen photos where people had used glow sticks to write words in the dark, and it was similar to what he was seeing now. Two fluorescent yellow spirals were rising and falling inside the glass container, twisting around one another.

'What are they doing?' Dad leant closer. 'They making some kind of pattern?'

Zak took a step forward, and the movement stopped. In an instant, and as one, the bugs smacked against the glass and stuck there like a solid wall of insects. Zak caught a glimpse of the grey, fleshy creatures inside the armour before a sharp pain flooded through his head.

POW!

The lab disappeared. Dad, the bugs, everything.

Like before, Zak was hanging in the air, and when he looked down, he saw an endless sea of blackness, but now he knew it wasn't a sea, but a hive of bugs stretching into eternity. And he knew if he fell into them, they would swarm over his body. They would smother him and he would drown in them as they ate him alive. In the seething darkness below, he saw the beginnings of a glowing yellow spiral. It turned and turned. Rising. Rising. A fluorescent double corkscrew reaching up and up towards him. He moved his arms, trying to float higher, to keep away from its reach, afraid of what it wanted, of what it would do.

'Zak? Zak?' Dad's voice was reaching out to him in the darkness. 'Zak?'

He turned towards the voice, feeling the comfort of its familiarity and *POW!* he was back in the lab, standing a few steps away from the glass container. Dad was frowning at him. 'You OK?'

Zak glanced at the container where the insects had now settled at the bottom. 'Yeah.'

'You zoned out for a minute. Like before. You sure you're OK?'

'Creeped out by the bugs,' he said.

'Mm-hm. Me too. Come on, we should go find Mum and May.'

'Yeah,' Zak agreed. 'Good plan.' He cast one more glance at the container of bugs.

'We'll check on Dima, then head over to Control,' Dad said as they reached the door at the end of the tunnel. But when they re-entered The Hub, they saw they weren't going to be able to do that.

Because Dima was gone.

OUTPOST ZERO, ANTARCTICA
NOW

'Dima?' There was still a dent on the cushion where the pilot had been sitting. His glass was lying on the floor, on its side, with water pooled around it. Close by were the remains of armoured insects, like the ones they had seen in the lab.

'I don't think these were here before,' Zak said. 'I mean . . . we'd have noticed, wouldn't we?'

'I don't know.' Dad put his arm around Zak's shoulder. 'Maybe not.'

'And why is it just the shell?'

'How do you mean?'

'Well, shouldn't there be something inside it? The grey yucky thing we saw in the lab?'

The two of them stood there, staring at the insect remains. This whole situation was turning out like one of the weirder *Jackson Jones* adventures, except actually being right in the middle of it was much scarier than reading about it.

'Come on, my young Padawan,' Dad said eventually. 'Dima didn't turn into a bug. He must be with Mum and May.'

'Yeah.' Zak took a last look. 'That must be it.'

At the far end of the Control Room there was a semi-circular bank of ten screens arranged in two rows of five. Right now, they displayed images fed from CCTV cameras around the base. In front of the screens, keyboards and unfamiliar electronic devices were neatly arranged on a long desk. Mum and May were sitting behind the desk in swivel chairs.

'Find anything?' May asked when Zak and Dad came in.

'Where's Dima?' Zak said, looking around. 'He's not out there. Where is he?'

'We haven't seen him.' Mum was confused. 'Not since we split up.'

'What about the cameras?' Zak pointed at the screens, but he could see the feed that was coming in from The Hub, and it was obvious that all four cameras in there were pointing away from where Dima had been sitting.

'Nothing works,' Mum replied. 'Well, the cameras are *on*, and they move from time to time, but none of the controls work.' To prove her point, she punched her fingers at a keyboard on the surface in front of her. 'See? Nothing happens. And that's not the only thing; none of the communications are working except for email, but–'

'Email Head Office, then,' Dad said. 'In Switzerland.'

'Totally tried it,' May replied.

'And?'

Mum put her elbows on the desk and rubbed her face with both hands. 'Where to start? OK, the email system seemed to be working, so I sent a message to Head Office explaining the situation. A couple of minutes later, they replied.' She pulled a keyboard towards her and brought the message up on screen.

To: outpostzero@exodus.com
From: hoffice@exodus.com
Subject: Outpost Zero Status

Dr Reeves
Thank you for your status update. Apologies for disturbing your holiday.
Everyone here is relieved to know that you have landed safely and that Outpost Zero operations are under control. Please keep us up to date with your findings on the drones.
And there's good news; the Project Leader has promised to refund the cost of your holiday!

Best wishes
Dr Ernest Hardy

Dad frowned. 'I don't understand. What did you send them? Why do they think everything's under control? How is our situation even *close* to being under control?'

'That's the thing.' Mum tapped the keyboard again. 'This is the email that went to them . . .'

To: hoffice@exodus.com
From: outpostzero@exodus.com
Subject: Outpost Zero Status

Please be advised that some systems are down due to adverse weather conditions, but everything is under control. Normal communications will resume as soon as we manage to get everything back to full operational capabilities.

Dr Evelyn Reeves

'. . . but that is *not* the email I sent. Not even close. I told them the *actual* situation, but somewhere between me writing it, and it leaving the base, the text of the email changed.'

'What do you mean *changed*?' Dad stared at the screen. 'How? Who changed it?'

'I don't know.'

'And why would they say everything's OK?' May asked. 'Everything *isn't* OK.'

'To stop them sending help,' Zak guessed. 'I mean, there's no need to send help if everything's OK.'

May stared at him like she was trying to get her head

round what he'd said; that someone was doing this – deliberately isolating them here in Outpost Zero.

'And that's not the strangest thing,' Mum said, 'because as far as I know, the only way to access this system is from Head Office in Switzerland, or from inside this room.'

'You think someone hacked into Head Office?' May asked.

'What for?' Mum pushed the keyboard away. 'It doesn't make sense.'

'Yeah, like everything else in this place,' Zak said. 'We found some weird insects in the lab; all pinned out and cut up. And there's a big glass container full of live ones and – all those bits on the floor? I think they come from the insects.'

'Insects?' Mum asked.

'See for yourself.' Dad handed the tablet computer to Mum and waited for her to scroll through the document. May stood and peered over her shoulder.

'They've been taking ice core samples?' Mum said.

'Looks like it.'

'Why? From where?'

Dad took off his glasses and pinched the bridge of his nose. 'Well, we're close to the Antarctic Chasm. Maybe they've been taking samples from *there*.'

'But Outpost Zero isn't equipped for that kind of operation,' Mum said. 'You need kit, personnel. These people are here to train for life on Mars, not to take core samples. And anyway, they couldn't find all this down there. All this . . . *life*. It's impossible.'

'That's what I said,' Dad agreed. 'We have to be reading it wrong. We're not biologists, we don't understand the data. There's no way it's from that deep in the ice.' He tapped the tablet screen. 'That would make it *old*.'

'How old?' May asked.

Dad raised his eyebrows. 'I'm no expert, but as far as I know, the ice in cores is usually thousands of years old. This, though? This looks more like *billions*.'

Mum put the tablet on the desk. 'I need to see these things.'

'Or maybe we need to find out what happened to Dima first,' May said. 'And everyone else. Maybe if we do that, we'll find out what's going on here.'

'You're right.' Dad sighed. 'Maybe Dima's with the others.' He dug his hands in his coat pockets, tapping his fingers against his hips. 'Wait a minute.' He stopped tapping and stood tall. 'Project members all have implanted microchips, don't they? So the Exodus Project can monitor their vital signs. Heart rate, blood sugar. They can be tracked. There should be a handset that–'

'Well, duh, Sherlock.' May crossed her arms. 'We already thought of that, but we can't find the handset.'

'You checked Medical and Science Two?'

'Yes.'

'OK, well . . .' Dad threw up his hands. 'You two stay here, see if you can get anything working. Zak and I will head to the Drone Bay; it's the only place left in the main part of the base. Without going outside, there's nowhere else they could be.'

'Right,' Mum agreed. 'But take one of those walkie-talkies.' She pointed to a row of handsets on the shelf to her left. 'They don't rely on these complicated comms, so they should work fine.'

'Makes sense.' Dad snatched two walkie-talkies from the shelf and checked they were on the same channel. He handed one to Mum and clipped the other to his belt. 'Stay in touch,' he said as he and Zak left.

OUTPOST ZERO, ANTARCTICA
NOW

As soon as he entered the North Tunnel, Zak stopped as if he'd hit a brick wall. His breath caught in his chest, and all he could do was stare.

The figure was back.

The same one he'd seen in The Hub, but this time there were no shadows to hide it. *This time* it was standing at the end of the tunnel, directly beneath the furthest spotlight. Clear as day. No mistake.

Well, not exactly clear as day. Because as Zak's breath came back to him, and he studied the figure, he thought there was something grey and vague about it; as if it were a shadow. Or a ghost. Or a–

Pain.

Sharp, clean, pain drove through Zak's head like a hot needle.

It lasted a fraction of a second, and was gone. The figure, however, remained where it was. The man – Zak was sure it had to be a man – was dressed exactly as he had been when he last saw him. The old-fashioned weatherproof jacket, the huge furry mittens, the hood, and the goggles that made him look like a giant insect.

'Do you . . . see something?' Dad whispered.

Zak opened his mouth to speak but his tongue was dry. His lips felt numb. 'See something?' he managed. 'Like what?' If Dad could see it, then he wasn't imagining this. It wasn't some crazy episode, like the doctors said he might get.

'I'm not sure.' Dad was still whispering. 'Like . . . a shadow. At the end of the tunnel?'

'You see it too?'

'I . . . I don't know. No. I thought there was something but . . .' Dad's voice trailed away as if he was trying to decide what he had or hadn't seen.

But Zak could still see it.

Right there.

The figure was no more than ten metres away but the more he stared at it, the more unclear he realized it was. The weatherproof coat was like ones he had seen in old photos on the Internet, of explorers standing on the ice, but there was no detail on it other than a few creases. The knee-length boots were dark grey, the hood was white, and the round goggles were filled with the blackest glass. The huge mittens were speckled black and grey and white. The figure didn't have any colour. Just like in those old photos.

It raised one hand, curling its fingers, beckoning to Zak.

Beckoning? Does it want me to go to it?

It stepped forward, arm extended, flickering like a dodgy image from a CCTV camera. There was movement beneath the woollen balaclava covering its face, as if it were speaking, but Zak couldn't hear its voice. And there was no sound as it moved. But there *was* a single flash of colour as the light caught on the surface of the goggles. A muddle of blue and red and green.

Like beetles' wings.

It's not there, Zak told himself. *It's not there. There's no such thing as ghosts. It's in my imagination.*

'Must be my imagination.' Dad's words echoed Zak's thoughts. 'I'm seeing things.'

But it was still there, moving towards Zak, one jerking step at a time, flickering as if it were trying to break through from another world.

'You don't see anything?' Zak's voice was a quiet whisper.

'No. Come on.'

'Dad . . .' Zak wanted to stop him, but Dad moved forward, on a collision course with the ghostly explorer, and–

It was gone. Just like that. The figure vanished as if it had never been there. The tunnel was as empty as the others had been.

'Dad?' Zak stared at the far end of the tunnel. 'Tell me what you saw. When we first came in.'

'Nothing.'

'Tell me.' Zak insisted. 'Tell me what it was. *What did you see?*'

Dad stopped and turned to him. He tightened his lips and fixed his eyes on the floor. He shook his head before meeting Zak's gaze again. 'Nothing.'

'*Dad*.'

'All right. Look, I don't want to scare you, but . . . a shadow maybe. It felt like there was something there, but . . .' He turned towards the far door. 'But there's nothing there now, and I don't believe in ghosts so–'

'Ghosts? What made you say that?'

'It's just my mind playing tricks on me, Zak.'

'Except I saw something too.'

'*What*? Really?'

'Yeah. A shadow. Something . . . that wasn't there.'

Dad watched Zak as if he were expecting this to be a joke.

'I really did,' Zak said. 'I really *did* see something.'

Dad smiled. It was a sad and sympathetic expression, and Zak knew what it meant.

He thinks I'm imagining stuff. He thinks I'm going bonkers.

'A trick of the light,' Dad said. 'That's all. Probably our own shadows as we came into the tunnel. There's definitely *something* weird going on here, but there'll be an explanation, and I promise it won't be anything to do with ghosts.'

Yeah, not ghosts, Zak thought, *but something. Something* rotten.

As soon as Dad punched the button, the door to the Drone Bay slipped open to reveal a large, silent room beyond.

Dad went straight in, but Zak stayed in the doorway as if trying to break through an invisible barrier. The headache was gone, but this room gave him the strongest sense of something being *wrong*. Whatever had happened, it was somehow connected with this place. He scanned the room, searching for the figure he'd seen in the tunnel, but the Drone Bay was free of ghosts. For now.

White walls, white floor, white ceiling, the place was more like an operating theatre than a workshop, but there was still the faint smell of oil and electricity in the air, mingled with the metallic tang of hot steel. Zak could *taste* the Drone Bay.

In the centre of the room was a large disc about four metres in diameter that was used as an elevator to lower the Spider drones on to the ice below. When Outpost One – the base on Mars – was completed, the whole module would be a giant airlock to give the Spiders access to the surface of the planet.

Around the edges of the disc, spare parts were laid out in cabinets, and tools were arranged like surgeon's instruments on white benches. Wires snaked out from machines ready to be plugged into the Spiders, for diagnosing faults, and keeping them charged.

At the back of the room there were three large bays, each with a name stencilled on the wall above it in black paint. HAL, ROY, and ED – each of them named after a robot from one of Mum and Dad's favourite sci-fi movies. Right now, HAL and ROY were empty, but the bay with ED above it was home to something that was one of the most amazing things Zak had ever seen. And one of the scariest.

The Spider was slightly bigger than a two-seater Smart car, and was made of a flat oval casing about a metre and a half deep that housed the robot's 'brain'. On top of that, the bulk of its body was a ribbed dome, like a bloated tick that had filled itself with too much blood. It had four legs, each jointed in six places, giving it the look of a weird, grey metal spider. Close to the front, it had four narrow arms designed to accept interchangeable attachments. For now, the arms were tipped with pincers.

Right now, ED was in its 'down' position, body resting on the ground, jointed legs in an upside down 'V', arms retracted.

Everyone in the 'robotic world' knew about Drs Evelyn and Adam Reeves because they had designed robots for researching the Mariana Trench, deep under the Pacific Ocean. So when the Exodus Project asked them to design something for *them*, Zak's mum and dad created some of the most sophisticated robots the world had ever seen.

Transfixed by the Spider, Zak could hardly believe three others like it were already on the surface of Mars, preparing Outpost One. Zak imagined them moving through the orange dust like aliens, conjuring new components from their 3D printers as if by magic, and putting them together to build a new base.

'We've got another problem,' Dad said.

'Hmm?' Zak was so busy staring at the metallic monster, he hadn't noticed he was already halfway across the room. A few more seconds and he would have been face to face with the Spider. He blinked hard, not quite sure how he had got there.

Behind him, Dad had the walkie-talkie to his mouth, his thumb pressing the 'talk' button. In fact, he was pressing it so hard the pad of his thumb had gone white.

'What is it?' Mum's distorted voice came through the walkie-talkie. 'Did you find Dima?'

'No. And there's something else. Hal and Roy are missing.'

'Say again. It sounded like you said "Hal and Roy are missing".'

'That's exactly what I said. Ed's here, but the other two are gone.'

'Nothing on the system?'

'No response at all.' He tapped at the tablet computer in his hands. 'Everything's dead.'

There was a pause, then Mum said, 'We're on our way.'

'So, this is bad?' Zak couldn't take his eyes off the Spider. 'They should all be here?'

'Seems like everything's disappearing.'

'Maybe that's where everyone is? They're out practicing with the drones?' Zak watched the Spider resting in its bay like a monster sitting in its lair. There was something ugly about the way it sat there. Like when you find the crusty remains of a spider in the corner of the shed.

The door swished open and Mum came in with May right behind her. 'Anything?'

'Nothing,' Dad said. 'Ed's powering-up but all the controls are dead.'

'He's powering-up on his *own*?'

'Someone else must be controlling him.' Dad's fingers tapped icons on the touchscreen. 'I have no idea where the other two are. All the cameras are off-line, all the read-outs are flatlining . . . I can't get any response.'

Mum watched the Spider. 'Where are your brothers?'

He? Him? Brothers? Zak shivered. *Yuck. As if they weren't creepy enough already, without Mum and Dad treating them like they were alive.*

Ed sat there while Mum and Dad started with their foreign-sounding technical speak. It was all 'normalize' this, 'autonomous' that or 'kinematic' the other.

'It's freaky, isn't it?' May came over and whispered in Zak's ear.

'It's not the only thing.'

'Hey, you.' She slapped his arm.

'I didn't mean *you*; I meant everything that's happening here. The lights, the people, the plane, those bugs in the lab . . .'

'We should've stayed in St Lucia.'

'Yeah, you're not wrong about that.' Zak's gaze was drawn to the Spider once more.

There was something glistening within the complicated joints and limbs. Zak frowned and put his hands on his knees, leaning down to see the Spider's underside where sinewy grey strands threaded backwards and forwards among the movable parts. Each strand disappeared into the oval casing that contained what Mum and Dad called its 'brain', but the strands weren't mechanical – and they definitely weren't wires. They looked more like something *biological*. Like something fleshy was growing on the Spider's brain. Or growing out of it.

Was that supposed to be there? He didn't think so. It looked like–

All at once, and with more speed than he could have imagined, the Spider came to life. With a quiet mechanical whir of parts, its legs extended, raising the body off the ground, the arms lifted as if they were ready to attack, and it came forward.

Tick-tack-tick-tack, its metal feet sounded on the floor. *Tick-tack-tick-tack,* as it came right at him.

Startled, Zak tried to get away but fell backwards, sprawling on to the circular platform. The Spider kept coming, huge and horrific, stopping only when its whole body was standing over him. It tilted forward so the dark lenses of its cameras were staring into Zak's eyes. Metallic arms reached out towards him, the nimble pincers coming straight for his face. Glistening, fleshy sinews twisted around the rods and wires of its joints, tightening and relaxing with the Spider's movements.

Behind him, May screamed.

'Stop him!' Mum shouted. 'Turn him off!'

Instinctively, Zak threw his arms up to his face for protection. Cold pincers touched his hands, and in that instant he knew why they couldn't find anyone at Outpost Zero. He knew what had happened to Dima. This Spider had killed them all. It had torn them apart.

And now it was going to do the same to him.

NOVEMBER ISLAND, INDIAN OCEAN
10 HOURS AGO

The Sikorsky MH-60S Seahawk helicopter came in low across the foam-crested waves. Reaching the coastline of November Island, it thundered over the narrow stretch of white sandy beach, and skimmed the jungle canopy as it headed inland.

To anybody who noticed it, November Island was unremarkable. It was charted only on the most detailed maps, and any keen-eyed kid with a love of scrutinizing Google Earth images wouldn't bother to take more than a second glance at it. Even to the most experienced analyst, it was nothing more than one of the many beautiful spots of sand

and jungle that lay in the warm waters of the Indian Ocean.

The unassuming spit of teardrop-shaped land was only one and a half kilometres long from end to end, and one kilometre across its widest point. It would take the average person no more than an hour to stroll around it. However, very few 'average' people visited the island, because if they did, there was a strong chance they would be dead in less time than it would take for them to walk those beautiful beaches.

November Island could only be reached by boat or helicopter, but both were restricted. Every centimetre of the emerald jungle, and the idyllic beach surrounding it, was monitored for intruders. Any boat that approached, perhaps carrying adventurous tourists hoping to discover a deserted island, would be met by a security patrol and turned away with a polite word. Those who ignored the polite word would either disappear without trace, or would be found far out at sea, victim to an unfortunate boating accident.

Inside the Seahawk helicopter, Larisa Lazarovich sat with her carefully selected team of operatives. She flicked through images and files on a tablet computer, double-checking the details Phoenix had sent her several hours ago. Lazarovich was a highly-skilled soldier, and her mission success rate was one hundred per cent. Only one of The Broker's operatives – a man named Thorn – could beat her record of twenty-eight successful missions. This was to be Lazarovich's twenty-ninth mission, and she did not intend to fail. The Broker did not like failure, and nor did Lazarovich.

During her first mission for The Broker, when she was twenty-one years old, Lazarovich had led a team into the Amazon jungle to recover valuable documents from a crashed plane. Only one of the team had objected to having a young woman as his leader, so Lazarovich made an example of him. She challenged him to a knife fight, during which she cut him badly, then left him to die. Now his bones were picked clean and scattered across the jungle.

No one ever again questioned her ability to lead a successful mission.

As soon as she detected the helicopter slowing down, Lazarovich pocketed the computer, unclipped her safety harness and stood up. The other operatives followed suit, two of them moving to the side doors and pulling them open.

The pilot said one word. 'Clear.'

Immediately, the operatives dropped two coiled ropes from each side of the aircraft, and rappelled to the grass below. The instant their boots touched the ground, they sprinted across the clearing and disappeared into a large concrete hangar concealed on all sides by thick jungle. The hangar's roof was camouflaged from the air by a photo-realistic mesh of images blending seamlessly into the trees. Even from the helicopter, close as it was, the hangar was invisible.

Lazarovich was the last to leave the aircraft, and when she had landed safely, the ropes withdrew into the helicopter, the doors slid shut, and the Seahawk turned and headed away from the island at top speed.

Inside the hangar, the operatives hustled over to the two prototype Osprey aircraft waiting with their pilots already prepared for take-off. On the floor, between the seats in the passenger cabin of each of aircraft, sets of kit were laid out in preparation for the team's arrival. Thermal clothing, Arctic camouflage, combat helmets, snow boots, webbing and state-of-the-art HK 416 A5 Heckler & Koch Carbines. As requested, Lazarovich's kit also included a XM25 grenade launcher – 'in case of emergencies'.

As soon as all the operatives were on board, Lazarovich spoke into her headset.

'Team is green.'

On that order, Land Rovers towed the aircraft out into the clearing and the engines started up. With tremendous noise, the Ospreys rose vertically from the jungle floor, pausing when they were several metres above the canopy of trees. They hovered as they rotated to face south, then the engines tipped forward and they flew out across the sea.

From the moment the Seahawk had arrived, to the moment the Ospreys were out of sight, less than five minutes had passed. A brief disturbance of noise and activity before November Island returned to being an uninhabited spit of land.

Lazarovich and her operatives weren't even ghosts. It was as if they had never been there at all.

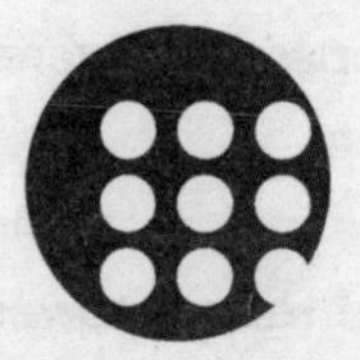

OUTPOST ZERO, ANTARCTICA
NOW

Last term, one of the kids in Zak's school died. It happened on a Saturday, so on Monday they had this big assembly. Mrs Thompson, the head teacher, told the whole school what happened, and lectured them about how they had to be careful when they went to the coast. The sea was dangerous, she said, and when it was cold like that, it could shock you and you'd drown.

Zak already knew all that stuff, everyone did, but Jason Crowley from Year Six must have thought he was indestructible or something, because one Saturday in October when he was messing about on the harbour wall, he got this crazy idea it would be fun to jump in. The cold shocked him, making him take a deep breath – except instead of breathing air, he breathed cold, salty sea water. After that he went under and didn't come back up. The lifeboat crew found him that evening, but it was way too late for Jason Crowley.

On the way to Mrs Coulson's maths class after assembly, Krishna Gopal told Zak that when you drown, your whole life flashes in front of you. Properly, he said. Every second of it. In fact, any sudden death was the same according to Kris. He told Zak you see it all in slow motion, playing out like a film.

Zak had never doubted Kris's words, but as the Spider loomed over him, its pincers lightly touching his hands, Zak's short life did not flash through his mind. Nu-uh. Not at all. There were no happy visions for Zak Reeves in his dying moments. Instead, he started to drown, but it wasn't cold sea water that washed over him, it was emotion. Strong and suffocating emotion, flooding like a tidal wave.

Terror, guilt, sadness, joy, jealousy – every emotion he'd ever had.

Then, as suddenly as it had begun, the flood of emotion stopped. The turmoil was replaced by the same queasy, floating feeling he'd had before. He was hanging in the darkness again, and he didn't dare look down because he knew what he'd see: the seething ocean of a billion insects. And it felt like something was watching his thoughts, feeling his emotions, crawling across his brain. The ache pulsed behind his right eye, throbbing like a fresh bump on the head, and Zak had the strongest sense something was examining what grew there. The ache intensified, then faded as the invader searched deeper into his mind. Zak tried to move, but his body refused to do what he wanted. His arms wouldn't budge, his legs were frozen in place, his head was filled with white noise and . . .

It's trying to tell me something. The thought struck him like a sudden slap in the face. *It isn't attacking me. It's trying to tell me something important.*

No, not something important. This was way beyond important. It was crucial. It was monumental. It was world-changing.

But it didn't know how to tell him. There were no words; there was just white and black and . . .

Ice.

Something buried deep inside ice. Something old. Something lost. No; something that was *hiding.* And it was calling to Zak, not saying his name exactly, not with words, but it was calling to him all the same.

'– away from him!' Mum's shrieking commands cut through the white noise filling his mind. There was a *whoosh* and a *pop* as the world came back to him and he opened his eyes to see the Spider still standing where it had been when he last saw it – legs taut, arms ready, body tilted towards the spot where he had been lying.

Everything else in the room had gone crazy. Somewhere behind him, Mum was shouting and hammering at the control tablet. May was yelling at the top of her voice, and Dad was dragging him by the shoulders, pulling him across the floor to the side of the room.

'I've got you. It's OK. It's OK,' Dad kept saying over and over again.

'Is it alive?' Zak was breathing hard. 'What was it doing?' The unreachable image of something important lost in the ice was fading.

'No, it's not alive,' Dad said. 'That's impossible.'

'It's not supposed to be.' May rushed to her brother's side. 'But what if it is? And where are the others? Maybe they *did* something.'

In the centre of the room, the Spider came to life once more, tilting back and swivelling in their direction.

'What's it doing?' Zak got to his feet.

Mum stabbed at the control tablet again. 'It's not responding to anything.'

'This is *not* cool,' May said. 'Literally. We have to get away from it.' She grabbed Zak's sleeve and dragged him towards the door. 'We're not staying in here.'

'You're right,' Dad agreed. 'You two go back to The Hub. We'll try to figure out what's going on.'

'Seriously?' May hit the button and the door slid open. 'You want to stay in here with that thing? And you want *us* to go out *there* on our own? There are two more of those things, remember? They must've done something to the people here. And what about Dima? Have you forgotten about him?'

'Of course not, but we need to–'

'Wait,' Mum said. 'He's doing something.'

Halfway out of the door, Zak glanced back to see the

Spider lower its body, the intricate leg joints shifting its weight.

'He's going into a cycle,' Mum said. 'How is that possible? It must be receiving instructions from somewhere.'

As she spoke, a high-pitched whirring came from the Spider, and it began to move its body in quick, jerking movements. Its legs remained strong and stationary, keeping it stable, and it was moving at such speed, it was almost impossible to detect the tiny changes in direction, but Zak knew what it was doing. He'd sat at the kitchen table at home, watching videos of it doing this, Mum and Dad showing it off like proud parents.

The Spider was printing something.

'What is it?' Mum said. 'What's he spinning?'

Spinning? Yeah, that's about right. Like a spider spinning its web to catch a fly. Except we're the flies.

'I can't tell.' Dad couldn't take his eyes off it as he returned to where Mum was standing. They were lost to it now; the way Zak and May had seen them lost to their work so many other days of his life.

'Let's get out of here.' May nudged her brother.

On the underside of the Spider's body, the stinger-like printer head was moving so quickly it was a blur, as if the monster was conjuring objects out of thin air. Beneath it, where Zak had been lying a couple of minutes ago, there were now two discs, no larger than a ten-pence piece. Beside them, a series of electronic components that could have been ripped out of a smartphone or a games console. As the printer continued to spin tiny new parts, the Spider's arms retracted, selected two fine attachments, and began fixing the components together. Fine wisps of smoke snaked up from it, and there was a vague smell of burning.

May tugged at the back of her brother's coat. 'Zak, let's go.' She raised her voice. 'Mum. Dad. *Please*. I'm scared.'

Mum approached the Spider. 'Just a second, sweetie. We need to . . .' Her words trailed off. 'Adam, what does this look like to you?'

Dad went to join her, crouching to get a better view of what the Spider was building. 'It looks like . . . I'm not sure. Is he building . . .? No, it can't be. We don't even have blueprints for something as sophisticated as this.'

As the Spider continued to assemble the parts, the high-pitched whirring stopped and the needle-like printer head retracted back into its underside. The room was overcome with an eerie silence. The only sound was the gentle *tick tick tick* as the spider fitted the components together.

'It's building *itself*,' Zak said. 'A small version of itself.'

'Can't be,' Mum told him. 'That's impossible.'

Impossible? That was a word Zak had heard too much since arriving at Outpost Zero. But he was beginning to think anything was possible.

The Spider's arms jittered and flicked at incredible speed, and within less than a few minutes of starting, it stopped. It didn't step back or sit or crouch, it just *stopped*.

They all stayed exactly as they were.

No one said anything until May broke the silence. 'Can we please go. Like, now?'

But Mum and Dad weren't listening. They were scientists

– robotic engineers – and they had witnessed something they had never seen before. Their robot had built a smaller version of itself. Now it had their undivided attention.

'Hey!' May shouted at them. 'We're *here*. Right *here*. Zak and me. Forget about your stupid robots for a minute and think about us!'

The small version of the Spider tapped its legs on the smooth surface of the lift. *Tick-tack*.

'Wait. Did you see that?' Mum asked.

'I saw it,' Dad replied.

'Mum!' May shouted again. 'We're literally standing right here!'

The small legs tapped again, one at a time, and the tiny monster began to move forward. Slowly at first, but gathering speed. It made a beeline for Dad who stood there, transfixed as it scuttled towards his foot. But it didn't stop there. As soon as it reached him, it gripped the front of his boot and began to climb.

That's when Dad started to back away. He lifted his leg, shaking it, trying to get the scuttler off, but it clung to the coarse fabric of his boots and continued to clamber higher. Dad slammed his foot down, dislodging the creepy robotic-spider-thing. It swung to one side, losing its grip, and skittering away across the floor. Before it came to a stop, though, it righted itself, planted its feet and headed for Dad once more.

Tick-tack-tick-tack. The noise was so horrible. *Tick-tack-tick-tack*.

The way the scuttler moved was so *lifelike*. It reminded

Zak of a spider scurrying across the carpet, heading for a dark place. But this thing wasn't trying to escape; it was fixed on attacking Dad, and there was no sign it was going to give up.

May was out of the door faster than Zak had ever seen her move. Zak was close behind her, Mum and Dad too, but the scuttling robot was catching up. Behind it, in the centre of the module, the drone was spinning up for a second cycle and Zak had a feeling that soon there would be two of these little monsters to deal with.

Full of confusion and fear, Zak chased May along the tunnel, glancing back to see Mum and Dad make it out of the Drone Bay. Mum stopped to watch as Dad slammed his fist on the button and the door swished shut. But he was a fraction of a second too late.

The scuttler slipped through the gap as the door closed, and it jumped. It travelled at least a metre through the air and landed on Dad's thigh. Immediately, it was on the move again, scurrying up his trousers, heading for the hem of his jacket and the dark safety beneath.

'Get off!'

Zak had never seen Dad so scared.

'Get off!' He swatted at his leg, swiping the thing away. Once again, it hit the floor with a quiet *ting*. Its legs skittered as it flipped itself over, but this time it wasn't quick enough. It had fallen close to Mum and she brought her boot down on it with a satisfying *crunch*.

'Got it.' She lifted her foot and inspected the tiny broken robot on the pale blue floor.

'Is it . . . dead?' Zak wasn't even sure it had ever been alive.

'Who cares?' May opened the entrance to The Hub. 'Just leave it and let's get out of here.'

But they couldn't get out of there; that was the problem. There was no way for them to leave, and there was nowhere for them to go. They were trapped and alone. In the middle of nowhere.

And from inside the Drone Bay came the high-pitched sound of the Spider going into a third cycle.

OUTPOST ZERO, ANTARCTICA
NOW

The four of them stood in The Hub, staring at the closed door leading to the North Tunnel.

'That thing was going to kill Zak.' May moved close to her brother and did something that surprised him – she put both arms around him and hugged him. 'We need to get out of here.'

She held him so tight Zak could hardly breathe, but he didn't object because he could feel her trembling. She needed the hug more than he did. When she broke away, he saw her black eyeliner was smudged and the colour had drained from her face.

'You're right,' Dad said. 'But if– Wait.' He stopped. 'Why didn't we think of this before? There are rules in place to protect data on the base; emails, documents, CCTV recordings . . . everything's uploaded to the servers and to Head Office in Switzerland–'

'Yes,' Mum interrupted, 'But we can't access any of the systems and we can't get in touch with Head Office. It's not as if we haven't tried.'

'But there's something else,' Dad said. 'Every day, the base uploads a back-up copy of the data on to an independent system. Something that *isn't* connected to the main systems. ViBac.'

'ViBac?' Zak asked.

'The Virtually Indestructible Back-up System,' Mum said. 'That thing is fireproof, waterproof, able to withstand extreme cold; it's . . . well, it's virtually indestructible.'

'So?' May said. 'How will that help?'

'So there might be something on there that can tell us what happened. Everything gets uploaded to it. *Everything*.'

'They keep it here.' Dad went to the far wall and tapped the map still stuck there. 'It's no more than a hundred metres. We'll be fine.'

Zak came closer to study the map. From a door at the back of The Hub, an open walkway crossed the ice at an angle between the North and East Tunnels. It led to a building labelled as 'Refuge'. There was also a set of steps at the far end, like a fire escape leading down to the ice.

'Some of the buildings are kept separate,' Dad said. 'In case anything happens to the rest of the base.'

'Like what?'

'Fire. That kind of thing. Refuge is basically a last resort. A self-contained area that isn't directly connected to the base.'

'Last resort?' May said. 'So maybe *that's* where everyone went? Dima too?'

'Maybe,' Dad agreed. 'Apart from Storage and Power, there's nowhere else they could be.'

'And you're sure it's no more than a hundred metres?' Zak asked. 'It's proper freezing out there.'

'Then we'd better wrap up,' Mum told him.

Zak pulled on his gloves, secured his hood and tightened the scarf across his mouth in preparation for the sub-zero conditions outside. While the others finished doing the same, he pressed his face against the small window in the top of the door and peered out along the walkway. 'Still windy out there,' he said.

'Let's just get it done.' May kept glancing at the door to the North Tunnel a few paces to her left. 'Right now, anywhere feels better than here.'

'Everyone ready?' Dad pulled on his goggles and looked back at them.

'No,' Zak and May said in unison.

Dad hit the button and when the door swished open, wind rushed into The Hub.

'Keep hold of the railing,' Dad said. 'I'll go first, then Zak, then May. Evelyn, you bring up the rear.'

'Right behind you, little brother.' May's mouth was hidden

beneath her scarf so her words came out muffled. 'Try to stay on your feet.'

'And you.' Zak stepped out on to the walkway and peered down at the ice several metres below.

'Keep going,' May told him. 'Don't stop.'

Exposed to the intense cold, Zak held tight to the railing and followed Dad. The walkway groaned and creaked under their feet. The wind was still strong, but the worst of it had passed, and in the hazy glow from the base lights, Zak could see the structures of Outpost Zero and the immediate land around them.

To his left was the North Tunnel – blue on the outside as well as the inside – and the red Drone Bay at the end of it. It looked bigger than it had seemed when he was inside, and there was something unreal about it, like it was a model, or a special effect from a movie. Ahead, Refuge was also red. Close to the buildings the base lights reflected from the icy white landscape, creating a cocoon for Outpost Zero, but further away the light faded to a crushing darkness. The kind of darkness that inspired fear.

Zak had known they were isolated, but for the first time since arriving, he could actually *see* how isolated they were. And now it felt more intense. Heavier. Like it was weighing down on him.

May tapped him on the shoulder. 'All right?' She showed him a gloved thumbs-up, so he returned the gesture.

Before they reached the end of the walkway, they passed a set of steps on the right, leading back down to the ice, then a few seconds more and they were there, at the door to one of the last places Dima and the others might be. Dad hit the button on the door and went into Refuge, switching on the lights. He pushed back his hood and pulled the scarf and goggles away from his face. 'It's this way.'

They filed along a short corridor, passing a couple of storerooms filled with cans and boxes, and a tiny room with a single bed pushed against the wall.

'Here it is.' Dad went into a small version of the Communications room – complete with computers and keyboards and radio equipment. All the screens were blank.

Dad moved the chair and tapped a bright orange box under the desk. 'Meet ViBac.'

ViBac was made of metal and looked heavy. It was about the size of a two-drawer filing cabinet, and had no buttons or lights on it, just a single USB-C port. It took Mum a matter of seconds to connect it to a laptop that was on the desk, and after a short wait, an icon for the ViBac appeared on screen. Mum double-clicked. As simple as that, and a window popped open on the laptop, with a list of folders. Right at the bottom of the list was a single video file.

'That was yesterday.' Zak pointed at the screen. 'Open that one.'

Mum clicked the file and the screen went black. A time-code appeared in the top left corner with the date from two days ago. After a couple of seconds, an image came into focus and Zak watched as the camera swept around The Hub.

It was different. The room *he* knew was deserted and bloodstained, like something out of a bad dream, but on-screen it actually looked normal – like it was a half-decent place to hang out. There was a hubbub of voices in the background and the occasional *clacking* sound. As the camera swept the room, Zak saw that the sound was coming from a game of pool between a man and a woman. They were both dressed in blue tracksuits, each with a white stripe running down the right side. Their names were printed on the chest, but the image wasn't good enough for Zak to read them. A boy, sixteen or seventeen years old, with his hair cut short like a soldier's, was leaning against the table, drinking from a can of Coke. He was also wearing a blue tracksuit.

'Nice outfits,' May muttered.

When the camera focused on the boy, he lowered the can and said, '*Get lost, Diaz. You should be long gone by now.*'

'*They just can't bear to leave us.*' Someone spoke off-camera, and the operator – Diaz, Zak guessed – swivelled round, taking in more of The Hub.

There were other people there; sitting at the tables, chatting, eating. A couple of teenagers were lounging on the L-shaped sofa playing a video game.

The camera settled on a woman standing in the kitchen, stirring a hot drink. '*You need to go*,' she said. '*Twenty-four hours outside the bowl, remember? The sooner you leave, the sooner you get back. Magpie's waiting.*'

'That's Commander Miller.' Dad pointed at the woman on screen. 'Diaz and someone else must be on their way out of the bowl for a collection trip. It's standard stuff – everyone has to learn to survive in the MRV for a twenty-four-hour period, as if they're going out to collect samples on Mars. "Out of the bowl" means outside this area – the base is in a kind of a bowl, but there's one shallow side where you can get up and out.'

'And who's Magpie?' Zak asked.

'Not who,' Dad replied. 'What. "Magpie" is what they call the MRV. It's a scientist joke. Magpies are supposed to like collecting stuff.'

Scientist humour. Yeah, ha ha.

The camera panned further round until it focused on a middle-aged, fair-haired man with a close-cut beard. He was dressed in ECW gear, and standing by the front door of The Hub. The camera zoomed in on the name printed on the chest of his jacket.

Peters.

'*You all set to go, Prof?*' Diaz spoke with an Australian accent but her voice was muffled. Peters gave her a thumbs-up, and she turned the camera on herself. Zak saw a close-up of it reflected in the tinted lenses of her goggles. '*Oh. Wait a minute.*' The camera pointed at the floor for a few seconds, then raised to focus on Diaz's face. No goggles this time. '*Here I am!*'

Zak was surprised to see that Diaz was the girl from the photos in the living quarters. He guessed she was about fourteen, with olive skin, short dark hair, and eyes that twinkled when she spoke. He couldn't imagine why anyone that age would want to be involved in something like the Exodus Project, but she appeared to be enjoying herself, smiling and waggling her eyebrows at the camera. '*Sofia Diaz reporting for duty*,' she said. '*And they told me I'd never amount to anything. Well, look at me now, Mr Allen, I'm part of a* mission. *And guess what, sucker? I'm going to Mars. My only regret is that you poor Earthlings are going to have to manage without me. Later, losers!*'

'Scan forward,' Dad said, so Mum moved the slider along the bottom of the screen.

In fast-forward, Zak saw a shot of the Magpie on the ice and a stack of gear piled beside it. It was dark and there were pools of light spilling out from the base, flooding across the ice. A brief blink and the gear was gone, and Peters was climbing aboard the Magpie. After a sweeping shot of The Hub, the video blinked again and Mum let it play.

'*Looks small from here*.' It was Sofia Diaz again.

The screen was mostly dark apart from a fuzzy light in the centre, towards the bottom. When the camera focused, the fuzzy light sharpened and separated into a number of small lights.

'That's Outpost Zero,' Dad said. 'She's filming the base from way out on the ice.'

The camera lingered on the lights. '*A few more weeks and we won't even be able to get a plane in here,*' Diaz said. '*Imagine that. It'll be so cold, the fuel will turn to gel. We could be on our own for months.*'

'Wait.' May reached forward and paused the video. 'Did she just say they won't be able to get a plane in here?'

'Don't worry,' Dad reassured her. 'We'll be long gone by then.'

'But you never said anything about that. You never said anything about not being able to leave.' May put back her head like she was trying to stay calm. 'Ugh. This just gets better and better.'

'We're going to be fine,' Mum told her. 'We still have weeks before it'll be that cold. Please. Panicking won't help. Let's just watch this and find out what we can, shall we?'

'And on the bright side,' Zak said. 'If we get stuck here, you won't have to go back to school. Just think – no more Vanessa Morton-Chandler.'

May looked at Zak like she was about to lose it, but finally she took a deep breath and nodded slowly. 'All right. Just play the video.'

Mum tapped the pause button and the screen jerked back into life.

Feels like we're a million miles from anywhere,' Diaz said, and Zak thought there was something comforting about her slow and considered accent.

'*We* will *be when we're up there*.' It was the first time Zak had heard Peters' voice. He sounded like he was from Scandinavia.

The image tilted to reveal a clear sky filled with more stars than Zak thought possible. '*You think there's anyone else up there? I don't mean on Mars – that's just Spiders building us a base – I mean further out*.'

'*Do you?*' Peters asked.

'*I dunno. I reckon there could be. But I'm starting to wonder what we've got down here*.' The camera swivelled, showing a glimpse of Peters as it swept around to take in the view of the icy desert. '*You know, since those guys from BioMesa turned up, I've–*'

'*We were told not to ask about that,*' Peters said. '*To not talk about it. If we do, it could jeopardize the whole project.*'

'*They're doing something out at The Chasm.*' Sofia ignored Peters. '*I've seen it.*'

'*You've seen it?*'

'*Yeah. I reckon they're taking the Spiders out there and lowering them in. Doing something they shouldn't.*'

'*I don't want to know.*'

'*Don't you? You don't want to know they're using the Spiders to drill core samples from way down? You don't want to know they found something under the ice? And I mean* deep *under the ice. You're a scientist, I thought you'd be interested . . .*'

'*Found something?*' The camera swung back and focused on Peters' face. '*Something like what?*'

'*Some kind of bug. Doc Blair's been looking at the core I gave him, and the thing I found inside it. An insect. Something–*'

'*Stop. Not on camera.*' Peters leant forward, his hand looming over the lens. There was a fumbling sound as the image blurred and flicked to a first-person view of a drive across the ice, the inside of the Magpie jolting about. Another flick and the image switched to a shot of two people walking away from the camera.

Dad leant over and paused the video. 'BioMesa? What were they doing here? And what were they doing with our

Spiders?' He took off his glasses and rubbed his nose before putting them back on. 'Sounds like she's talking about those things we found in the lab. Those insects, or whatever they are.'

'Insects deep under the ice?' Mum said. 'That no one has ever found before? How could–'

'Just play the video,' May said. 'Then we'll find out.'

When Dad unpaused it, Sofia and Peters continued walking away from camera. They used a small drill to put a hole in the ice, then waved to camera before coming back. For a few long seconds, the lens remained pointed at the spot until Sofia said, '*Fire in the hole*.'

There was a loud *crack* and a plume of ice shot into the air where they had been standing.

'They're blowing stuff up?' Zak asked.

'Small controlled explosions,' Dad said. 'It's all part of the collection process.'

Mum scanned the video forwards and more events passed in jerking, twitchy movements as Sofia and Peters went about the business of collecting samples to bring back to base. There was loads of footage like that until a sudden change made Mum stop and let the movie play at normal speed.

The screen was now filled with an image of Sofia's face. Her eyebrows were drawn together, her lips were tight, and her eyes were narrowed.

'*OK*.' She swallowed. '*My name is Sofia Diaz. From Australia. I'm the daughter of Professor Rosita Diaz and Professor Eco Diaz. The cameraman is Professor Valter*

Peters, from Sweden.'

'Norway. I'm from Norway.'

The camera turned around briefly to show Peters' concerned face, and Zak leant away from the screen as if expecting something bad to happen.

'Umm . . .' Sofia took a deep breath as soon as the camera was on her again. *'We might have some kind of problem. We're not sure, it could be nothing, but we checked in with Outpost Zero before bedding down – like we're supposed to – and Commander Miller said there were issues with power at the base. Outside comms not responding, lights and heat going off. Could be the weather but Mac was working on getting it fixed. Thing is, we tried to report in this morning and there's no answer. Radio's working fine, there's just no answer. It's . . .'* Sofia shook her head and her frown deepened. *'Storm picked up a right shocker in the night and she's been going for more than four hours now. We're getting worried so we're going to cut our trip short, come back into the bowl. Prof Peters . . . Sorry,* Professor *Peters and I are heading back to Outpost Zero now. We're a couple of hours out, maybe more in this weather, so we should be there by . . .'* She checked her watch, *' . . . sometime after midday.'* She stared into the lens for a while longer before her eyes shifted and she nodded to her cameraman. *'OK?'*

There was a brief blink and the screen was filled with an image of The Hub's interior. It was in total darkness except for the piercing white light mounted on the camera. On the top left of the screen, the timecode indicated the video was filmed about twenty-two hours ago.

'*This isn't right*,' Peters said as the camera panned around the room, illuminating and casting shadow. '*Not right at all*.'

The last time Zak had seen The Hub on screen it had been filled with people, but now it looked exactly as *he* knew it. Like the ship in his book – the *Mary Celeste*. Everybody was gone, and he could hear the storm raging in the background.

'*We've checked every module*.' Peters spoke to the camera. '*But there's no sign of them. Nothing. Power's down; no light or heat. I don't–*'

'*Hey, what about the tracker?*' The camera panned round to focus on Sofia's face. '*We can find them with that*.'

'*Good thinking*.'

'That's why we couldn't find it,' Mum said.

The video blinked again, and they were inside the Control room. Sofia was standing in front of the bank of computer screens, holding something the size of a smartphone. She stared right through the screen at Zak. '*Peters thinks we should keep recording. We don't know what the hell is going on here and, ugh, this is ridiculous, it feels like I'm in a horror movie or something. You ever see the one where the guys are isolated in–*'

'*Stick to what is important. The tracker.*'

Sofia sighed and lowered her eyes. '*Look, we're going to keep rolling on this because we don't know what we're going to find, and we don't know what's going to happen, so . . .*' She focused on the device in her hand. The camera moved closer, bringing the device into shot, and Sofia used her thumb to switch it on.

'The tracker,' Dad said.

The device came to life, and a satellite image popped into view. Mostly it was white, with a few patches of grey dotted here and there. Illuminated grid lines criss-crossed the image. Sofia pinch-zoomed in until the base came into view, the separate buildings clearly visible against the ice and snow. A second later, a collection of blue markers lit up, clustered together in one place.

'*We found 'em*,' Sofia said.

'*That's* all *of them*.' Peters focused the camera on the list of names beside the map. '*My family, your family . . . everyone. But what are they doing out there?*'

'*I dunno. Some kind of meeting?*' Sofia looked at the camera. '*I guess we'd better go and find out.*'

OUTPOST ZERO, ANTARCTICA
22 HOURS AGO

When Sofia Diaz was thirteen years old, she read an article in *Adventure Magazine* about a one-way trip to settle on Mars. The article described details about how the project would unfold, and was asking for families to apply. The Exodus Project was looking for highly intelligent, resourceful personnel seeking adventure.

Sofia knew, straight away, that she wanted to go. No, not that she *wanted* to go, that she *had* to go. That she was *supposed* to go. There was no question in her mind, she and her family were exactly the kind of people needed for the project.

Her papa, Professor Eco Diaz, was a well-respected expert in astrophysics. Born in Australia, he had worked on the space programmes in Russia, the United States and Great Britain. Sofia's mama, Professor Rosita Diaz was a biochemist working on groundbreaking techniques to grow plants in difficult environments. Sofia's brother, Pablo, was at university studying maths, which meant Sofia was the odd one out. At school, she was average across the board, but outside of school, every moment was spent seeking adventure. Scouts, rock climbing, kayaking, surfing, caving, even skiing – which wasn't easy when you lived in Australia. She could ride a dirt bike like a professional, and had already spent two years learning Wing Chun Kung Fu. Sofia was *hungry* for adventure, always pushing herself to the next thing, but she couldn't find anything that gave her quite the adventure she craved.

Until now.

It took her ages to persuade Mama and Papa to apply, and her friends told her she was mad. Two years training in Antarctica, followed by a six-month one-way space flight to settle on a dusty planet with a handful of other families wasn't their idea of fun. But Sofia felt as if it was her destiny. She wanted to do something no one had ever done before. And, as young as she was, she knew she had something to offer. She wasn't a science nerd, but she was smart, strong and resourceful.

Sofia Diaz believed she would be an asset to the Exodus Project, and now, at fourteen years old, and only two months into her training, was the chance for her to prove it.

The wind rose like a demon in the night and didn't let-up for hours. It howled across the ice, bringing with it a blizzard that turned the world into a blur. It made driving difficult, so she and Peters took three times longer than they should to reach Outpost Zero. Sofia insisted on driving the Magpie – she was better at it than Peters – but spent the entire journey going no faster than a crawl, with her nose centimetres from the windscreen. One wrong move could see them swallowed by a crevasse and never seen again, so she kept it slow and steady even though she was desperate to get back. Everyone she loved was at Outpost Zero, and she had a feeling they needed her help.

Arriving at the base was like coming into a ghost town. There was no power, the temperature had dropped, and The Hub carried the faint smell of overripe fruit and . . .

'Do you smell *fish*?' Sofia asked.

'I don't know,' Peters said. 'Could be.'

The smell stood out to Sofia because Antarctica was bland. Snow and ice don't smell of anything, and the extreme cold meant most objects held on to their aromatic chemicals. In the warmth of The Hub the most common smells were usually coffee, fried food and sweaty people.

When she noticed the fragments of insect casings littering the floor, Sofia immediately thought of her trip out to the BioMesa cavern, and how she had returned with Ice Core #31. Doc Blair's bugs.

That was when her first feelings of guilt began to form. Perhaps this was all connected to something she had done.

In the Control room, Sofia turned on the tracker and zoomed in on the base. Instead of there being blue dots scattered all over Outpost Zero, showing everyone going about their work, they were all focused in one place.

'We found 'em.' Sofia tried not to sound scared.

'That's *all* of them.' Peters focused the camera on the list of names beside the map. 'My family, your family . . . everyone. But what are they doing out there?'

'I dunno. Some kind of meeting?' Something wasn't right. 'I guess we'd better go and find out.' Sofia gave him a reassuring smile, but inside she was on full alert and fighting a rising sense of panic. 'I'm sure everything'll be fine.' She double-checked the fastenings on her coat, and tugged at her fur hat with the floppy dog-ears to make sure it was on tight.

As soon as they were both ready, Sofia lowered her goggles and opened the door. Feeling the full force of the blizzard, she put her head down and stepped out into the cold, holding on to the handrail as she scanned the area surrounding the base. There was nothing to see. No clues about what had happened there. The ferocity of the blizzard meant she could barely see more than a couple of metres ahead of her, and any tracks were long gone.

Far away, on the other side of the landing strip, the Storage Bay was invisible through the storm.

She handed the tracker to Peters. 'You OK, Prof?' She leant close to his ear and shouted over the howling storm. 'You ready?'

'Yes!' he shouted in return.

Sofia steeled herself for what was to come, and started down the steps, boots crunching ice as she battled her way over to the Magpie. Peters followed and waited, camera still running, as Sofia climbed into the vehicle.

When she emerged from the cabin, Peters pointed the camera at what she was carrying. 'You think we're going to need those?'

'Be Prepared. It's a good motto.' She shoved a bright orange flare gun into her jacket pocket. Into her other pocket, she stuffed a handful of refills. The second thing she had taken from the Magpie was a metal rod, about a metre and a half long, with a scoop on the end. It was designed for collecting rock samples, but Sofia figured it would pack a good punch.

'Here.' She handed it to Peters.

He backed away, now seeing it as a weapon rather than as a scientific tool.

'Take it,' she insisted.

Reluctantly, Peters put the tracker in his pocket and took the tool from her.

Sofia grabbed a second collection tool from the Magpie, along with a large coil of tough, light rope. She wrapped one end around the front driver's side wheel-axle, and secured it with a clove hitch knot, then put her arm through the rest of the coil. 'Do kids read Hansel and Gretel in Sweden?'

'I have no idea. I'm from Norway.'

'But you know the story, right?'

'Of course.'

'Well, this is our trail of breadcrumbs.' Sofia pointed a thumb into the blizzard. 'I reckon it's going to be rough out there; we need to know the way back.'

Peters eyed the coil of rope around Sofia's shoulder.

'Don't worry.' Sofia read his mind. 'It'll be long enough.'

The wind beat at them as if it wanted to wipe them from the Earth. It fought to get inside their jackets, and hooked its invisible fingers under their hoods, but they leant in to it and kept their heads down as they struggled across the landing strip, uncoiling the rope in their wake.

'Still getting that reading?' Sofia stopped to check on Peters.

Peters pulled the tracker from his pocket. 'It's stronger now.' He held it up for Sofia to see the blue dots pulsing over the spot where Storage lay. 'No sign of movement.'

Sofia checked the tension on the rope. 'When we get there, I want you to stay behind me.'

'Why? What are you expecting? I should go first, I'm the–'

Sofia didn't wait for him to finish. She was fit, strong and skilled at Wing Chun Kung Fu. Peters was smart, but he was short, light and on the wrong side of forty. If they were going to face any kind of physical challenge, she wanted to be the first to deal with it. Sofia knew that if she had to strike, she would strike hard, fast, and without hesitation. Professor Peters, on the other hand . . . well, not so much.

Sofia set off again, continuing until she came to the guide rope lining the far edge of the landing strip. Without even pausing to catch her breath, she ducked under the rope and trudged on through the blizzard. Another hundred metres and Storage loomed out of the storm.

When she reached the steps, Sofia secured her rope to the handrail so they could follow it back to The Hub later. Once that was done, she tightened her grip on the rock collection tool, and climbed the metal stairs as quietly as she could. Reaching the top, she wiped ice from her goggles and turned to the camera. 'OK. We're going in.'

'Wait,' Peters said. 'I should–'

She hit the button and stepped inside.

Peters followed her into the darkness, and the door swished shut behind them.

They stood motionless, listening, but there was nothing more than the muffled howl of the wind.

The first thing Sofia noticed was how warm and damp it was in there. The place was humid, way hotter than it was supposed to be on the base. There was a strong smell of sweat, like a locker room, with another scent lying underneath it; something sweet and ugly, like overripe fruit.

As her eyes grew accustomed to the darkness, she scanned the room, making out the silhouettes of the items she expected to see. Shelves laden with equipment, packing crates, spare parts, tools and–

Something new. Something she didn't recognize. Something that shouldn't be there.

It stood at the far end of the module, large and dark, hidden in shadow.

Sofia raised her weapon, holding it over her shoulder

like a baseball bat ready to swing. 'It's hot in here,' she whispered. 'There must be power to this part of the base. You know where the light switch is?'

'Yes,' Peters replied. 'I'll turn it on.'

'Not yet. Point the camera at the far end of the room and wait for my count of three. Then I want you to switch it on.'

'Why?'

'Please,' she said. 'Just do it.' And without waiting for an answer, Sofia began to count. 'One . . .

'. . . two . . .

'. . . three. Now!'

The lights came on as soon as Peters flicked the switch. They flared over the room, illuminating the shape skulking in darkness.

Except it wasn't just one shape. It was many shapes. Many people.

Many monsters.

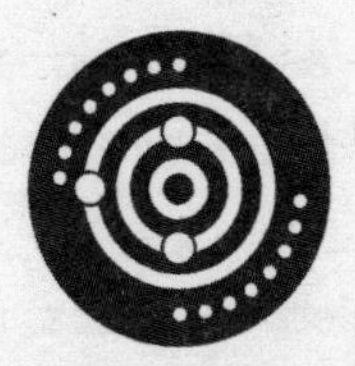

OUTPOST ZERO, ANTARCTICA
NOW

'Is that them?' Zak asked. 'Is that the people who are supposed to be *here*?'

Mum paused the screen, showing a large group of people standing to attention at the far end of the Storage Bay. Backs straight, arms by their sides, hands balled into fists, they were shoulder to shoulder in three rows of ten, and one row of eight.

'There's too many of them.' May cleared her throat. 'There's only supposed to be thirty-two people on the base.'

Zak counted them; thirty-eight. Forty including Sofia and Professor Peters. 'So, who are the others?'

He looked at Mum and Dad.

'BioMesa?' Dad suggested.

'Let's play the rest.' Mum tapped 'play'.

On-screen, Sofia dropped the collection tool and went straight to a man standing in the front row. *'Papa!'* Tall and olive-skinned, the man wore a red coat and a grey bobble hat. His eyes were closed, as if he were sleeping; his face was glistening with sweat. When Sofia shook him, he didn't respond at all.

'*Mama!*' Sofia pushed through to a woman in the second row, but again, there was no response. Beside her, Sofia's brother also remained blank when she shook him. '*Pablo! Wake up!*'

While Sofia struggled to get a response, Peters put down the camera and rushed forward, trying to wake a girl who was about thirteen years old. The name printed on her chest was 'Hilda Peters'. Blonde plaits fell from beneath the red and black beanie on her head. Beside her, a short woman, with a slight build, had the name 'Dr Eva Peters' printed on her jacket.

'Why are they just standing there?' May said. 'They're like . . . zombies. I mean, *literally* like zombies.'

They weren't rotting corpses, like in *The Walking Dead* comics May read, but she had a point – they did look a *bit* like zombies, but . . . 'They're breathing.' Zak leant closer to the screen. 'You can see them breathing.' He pointed at a man in the front row. The chest of his jacket was rising and falling with each shallow breath.

'So, what's wrong with them?' May whispered.

OUTPOST ZERO, ANTARCTICA
22 HOURS AGO

'What's wrong with them?' Peters said. 'Why won't they wake up?'

Sofia moved from her papa to her mama to her brother and back again, trying to get a response – any kind of response – but no matter how she tried, they stayed completely still. Their breathing was the only sign of life.

'What's wrong with them?' Peters was on his knees in front of his daughter. 'What's wrong with them?'

Sofia ignored his rising panic. She was too fixated on controlling her own. And beneath that, there was a creeping dread that this might be something to do with the core she had stolen. Core #31.

'Papa. Wake up. *Please*.' She stood close to him, watching his face, calling his name and–

He moved.

'Papa?'

Sofia's papa squeezed his eyes tight for a few long seconds, then opened them wide. There was something so *alive* in the way he looked at her. His eyes moved from side to side, round and round. They bulged and glistened as tears sprang into them. But other than that, he didn't move. *Couldn't* move.

'What is it, Papa?' Sofia spoke quickly. 'What are you doing? *What happened?*'

'He's trying to tell you something.' Peters came to Sofia's side and waved a hand in front of her father's face. 'Professor Diaz? What's going on? What happened here?'

To Sofia's left, Commander Miller opened her eyes. The man beside her did the same, and within a few seconds, the whole group had woken and were staring ahead.

'You trying to tell me something?' Sofia ignored the others and concentrated on her papa.

Peters returned to his wife and daughter, shaking them, waving his hand in their vision, trying to get a reaction.

As Sofia watched, her papa opened his mouth. A little at first, then wider and wider. His eyes bulged with effort, tears running down his cheeks. A sound came from him like air escaping from a limp balloon. His lips trembled as he tried to move them; tried to form words for his daughter to hear.

'What is it?' Sofia moved closer. 'What are you trying to say? What are you–'

Papa snapped his mouth shut, his teeth coming together with a *clack*. He squeezed his eyes in pain, then opened them with that creepy, bulging stare as he tried to move his lips and–

His face dropped as if all the muscles had been paralysed at once. His eyelids drooped, his mouth sagged, and his chin relaxed.

'What just happened?' Peters looked up at Sofia.

'I don't know. But I don't like it. There's–'

Then Commander Miller spoke. She opened her mouth and whispered two words.

'Help us.'

She paused before repeating the words.

'Help us.'

The third time she said it, Sofia's papa joined her, speaking the same words. His croaky whisper melting together with Miller's. Doc Blair, standing to her right, joined in too, and Dr Asan beside him. One by one, the others relaxed and began to speak until all thirty-eight of them were standing to attention with blank faces, repeating the same words over and over again.

'Help us. Help us. Help us.'

'Why are they saying that?' Peters backed away. 'Are they hypnotized or something?' The pitch of his voice was growing higher and higher. 'What the heck is going on?'

Sofia dared to step closer. She couldn't run away from this. She had to know. She waved her fingers in front of

Papa's face, but he didn't flinch. Instead, he closed his mouth and stopped speaking. Immediately, the others did the same, and everything fell silent.

With the sound of her own blood thumping in her ears, Sofia hesitated, leant closer, and looked into Papa's eyes. Seeing nothing, she pushed through to the second row of zombies and looked into Mama's eyes, then her brother's. Her mouth was dry and she trembled despite the heat, but she was trying hard to stay calm. She had every reason to freak out right now, but she was keeping it together. She *had* to keep it together. 'Maybe it's some kind of hypnotism. It's like they're . . . I don't know . . . in some kind of trance.' She turned and spoke directly to Peters. 'I don't know wha–' she stopped.

'What?' Peters asked. 'What is it?'

Now it was Sofia's turn to back away. 'What is *that?*' She glanced left and right. 'What is . . .? Oh my God. They've all got one.'

'One what?' Peters asked. 'What are you talking about?' But when he stepped past the front row of zombies and turned to see the back of their heads, he stopped with his mouth open, and stared.

OUTPOST ZERO, ANTARCTICA
22 HOURS AGO

Sofia was afraid, confused and curious all at once. There was a strange device stuck to the back of each person's neck – right in the centre, along the ridge of their spine. Mama, Papa, Pablo and all the other people she'd been living with for the past two months had one. People she was starting to think of as family. Even the BioMesa guys – including Jennings, whose access card Sofia had used to sneak into the research cavern.

She wiped sweat from her brow and leant closer to inspect the thing attached to Papa's neck. It was mechanical, but it looked *alive*. Like a small, fat spider with six spindly legs. There was a tiny trickle of dried blood where each leg had broken the skin, and as Sofia watched, the thing's legs shifted with the tiniest movements. Something grey and fleshy glistened in its intricate joints.

Sofia picked up the rock collection tool and gripped it tight. With the other hand, she reached out towards the spider thing. 'You think it'll come off?'

'Careful.'

She touched the thing with the tip of one gloved finger, withdrawing in a flash. The thing remained where it was.

Sofia removed her glove and touched it again. When it didn't react, she gripped it between her forefinger and thumb. 'It's warm,' she said. 'Feels like . . . I'm not sure . . . metal?'

'Not metal.' Peters kept his distance. 'Composite. Like the carbon composite the Spiders use for printing.'

'That grey stuff, though . . . it's like brain or something. It's disgusting.'

'It looks organic,' Peters said. 'Alive. Like living flesh.'

'Wait a minute.' Sofia leant closer. 'That bug I told you about?' (*There it was again – the feeling this had something to do with what she had stolen from the cavern.)* 'The one that came out of the ice core I took?' She tried to ignore the rising guilty feeling. 'Doc Blair cut one open, and its insides looked like this grey stuff.'

'What are you saying? That this is from an *insect*?'

'I dunno. I'm going to see if it comes off.'

'What if it hurts him?'

'We have to do something.' Sofia could see how afraid

Peters was – probably more afraid than *she* was. His face was covered with a sheen of sweat, his lips were trembling, and his breathing was heavy.

'I'm going to do it now,' Sofia said.

Peters nodded.

'OK.' She tugged gently on the strange parasite.

The skin on the nape of Papa's neck stretched back, as if the thing was going to come off with a wet *pop*, but its tiny joints flexed and the grey stuff flexed with them like muscle. The thing tensed its legs and gripped tighter, sharp feet digging deeper into Papa's flesh as it clung on.

Sofia let go immediately and stepped back. 'Did you see that?'

'It held on,' Peters said.

'Yeah. And did you see that needle or whatever it was?'

'No?'

'There's something coming out of its belly, and it's stuck into Papa's neck. Like a mosquito's needle.' Sofia shivered. 'Whatever it is, I reckon it's making everyone like . . . this. Could someone be doing it? Deliberately, I mean? Could someone be making these things and doing this?'

'You mean some kind of mind control?'

'I dunno. Maybe.'

'No.' Peters shook his head. 'That's impossible.'

Sofia moved to stand in front of Papa and look into his face. 'We'll find out what's going on,' she said to him. 'I promise. I'll get that thing off your neck and–'

Sofia stepped back and put a hand over her mouth.

'What is it?'

'There's something . . .' Her skin flushed red hot, bile rose in her throat, and cold washed over her. Every inch of her flesh tightened into goosebumps. In a second her blood went from boiling to freezing, and her insides contracted as if they were shrinking.

'What is it?' Peters said again as he came to her side.

Sofia couldn't take her eyes off the grey . . . *thing* . . . curled into Papa's right nostril. It was exactly the same colour and consistency as the sinews on the bug attached to his neck. Grey and glistening and translucent. Sofia had thought it looked like brain tissue but now, in her horror, something else came to mind. An image of shooting cans with her Black Widow catapult while Mama and Papa prepared food on the barbecue. The smell of charcoal burning, of sausages cooking. And lying on a plate beside the barbecue was a plate of raw prawns.

That's what it looked like. The thing inside Dad's nose – like the thing Doc Blair had cut from the black armoured bug – had the colour and consistency of an uncooked prawn.

The idea of it was ridiculous – *raw prawns? That's madness.* But Sofia couldn't shake the image. It tore her between terror and hysteria.

And then the thing moved. With one slick, fluid motion, it slid upwards, moving out of sight. Sofia was flooded with a crashing wave of nausea that broke the moment Papa opened his eyes.

His body loosened, his shoulders relaxed, and he stared right at his daughter.

Sofia recognized the panic that was building in her. She had seen cavers experience an overload of emotions when they thought they were stuck underground. She had seen them lose control of their thoughts and feelings, even their breathing, as their panic rose. So she fought it hard. She would *not* panic. She fixed her eyes on Papa's and forced herself to be calm.

Papa frowned. 'Join us.'

'Oh God.' Peters jumped back, almost dropping the camera.

The other people in Storage opened their eyes, all of them turning to face Sofia and Peters. They stood relaxed and did something that made Sofia's scalp tingle.

They smiled.

And then spoke again.

'Join us.'

'Papa?'

'Join us.'

They began to move. All thirty-eight of them shuffled forwards one step as if they had forgotten how to walk. They were hesitant, unstable, but the second step was more confident.

'Join us.'

Sofia backed away, but the people took another step. And as they did so, Papa raised his hands. When his arms were level with the ground, something slipped out from the narrow gap between his cuff and his glove. A black bug, a beetle-scorpion-earwig thing, about the size of her thumb. It scuttled towards Papa's elbow and circled round under his arm before another appeared. And another. And another.

'Join us,' Papa said to his daughter. 'Join us.'

Sofia retreated further as the people crowded around her, their fingers grasping at her coat, their muscles becoming stronger, their will becoming more determined.

Insects began to scramble out from the neckline of Papa's jacket. They scuttled to his shoulder, spread their wings, and took to the air.

'Go!' Sofia shouted at Peters. 'Get out!'

They turned and headed for the door.

Behind them, the settlers followed.

The door swished open as soon as Sofia hit the button. Ice and powdery snow blasted them like shrapnel, swirling into Storage. The crowd of zombies steadied themselves against the brute force of the weather, but showed no sign it bothered them. They continued to shamble forwards, reaching out to grasp Sofia and Peters, who had hesitated in the face of the storm.

'Get out!' Sofia shouted. 'Out!' She put both hands in the centre of Peters' back and shoved him hard into the blizzard.

She rushed out behind him, slamming her fist on the button, closing the door. As it swished shut, Sofia heard the awkward buzz and clatter of insects.

She stumbled down the steps, no idea if the settlers would continue to follow, but she had no intention of waiting to find out. 'Keep going!' she told Peters. 'Head for the guide rope.'

Neither of them dared look back, but they both felt the anticipation of what might come – of the door sliding open again, of the people shambling out into the blizzard.

But the door didn't open. The people didn't follow.

Something far worse awaited them in the storm.

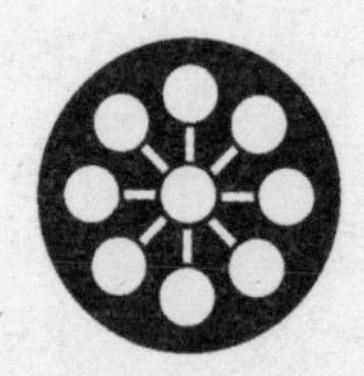

OUTPOST ZERO, ANTARCTICA
22 HOURS AGO

At the bottom of the steps, Sofia grabbed the guide rope and forged on towards the landing strip. It was impossible to see more than an arm's length in front of her, so the rope was her lifeline. Without it, she and Peters would lose their way; probably freeze to death a stone's throw from The Hub.

When Storage was lost in the storm behind them, Sofia stopped and leant close to Peters' ear. 'Give me the scanner.'

'What happened in there? What's going on?'

'Just give me the scanner!' Sofia had defeated her panic,

but she could see Peters was still battling with his. 'Quick!' She reached for his pocket, but he pushed her hand away and fumbled for it himself.

She took it from him, brushed ice crystals from the screen and squinted at the steady blue glow of the trackers on the satellite map. 'They've gone back to where they were,' she shouted. 'Come on, let's get out of this weather. And don't lose that camera.' She stuffed the tracker into her pocket.

As she battled through the storm, Sofia kept an eye on Peters and considered her options. Their priority had to be ViBac. It was essential they upload the video footage so if anything happened to them, there would be a record of this. Somebody would come looking for them, and they'd need to know what had happened here. After that, she had to call for help, so their best bet was to head to Refuge. Once there, they could–

'There's something out there!'

Peters' words sent a surge of adrenaline washing through her veins, and she turned to see him standing a few paces behind her. He was pointing the camera along the landing strip to their right.

Sofia wiped her goggles but all she could see was the swirling frenzy of particles in the wind.

'Something's moving.' Peters kept the camera pointed into the storm. 'Something big.'

'I don't see anything.' But as she said it, a darkness moved in the white-out. A large, grey shadow, shifting from left to right across her limited field of vision. And, barely audible over the storm, came the strange *tick-tack-tick-tack* of metal striking ice.

'You see it?' Peters called. 'You *hear* it?'

'I . . .' Sofia wiped her goggles again, wondering if it had been her imagination, a trick of the blizzard, but the shape moved again. This time it grew larger, becoming darker as if it were approaching. 'Keep moving.' She fought hard to hide the fear in her voice. 'Keep moving.' She wanted to stay strong for Peters. It was her job to stay strong. 'Just keep–'

The shadow surged forward, exploding from the blizzard like a shark erupting from the foamy sea. Sofia had never liked the erratic movements of the Spiders. The way their legs stuttered; the way their arms jerked when they swapped attachments, but when the Spider came at them out of the storm, it was different. The jerky movements were replaced by smooth, fluid motion. This thing wasn't like a robot now: it looked as if it were *alive*, and it came with the speed of an unstoppable juggernaut: a mass of scuttling legs and reaching arms.

When Sofia first realized what it was, she thought there was no way it was going to stop. It was going to trample right through them, crush them into the ice. But it *did* stop. In the blink of an eye, it came to a halt, centimetres from where Peters was standing.

Peters was too shocked to do anything more than stare in horror, camera still pointed at the Spider which leant forward as if it were inspecting him.

Sofia knew she had to do something, so she raised the

rock collector she had taken from the Magpie, and swung it as hard as she could. There was a crunch when it connected with the Spider. The impact of metal on metal jolted her arm, and rattled her teeth.

Taken by surprise, the Spider paused only for a heartbeat before it struck. With an unnatural pounce, it extended one of its arms and snatched hold of the rock collector as Sofia swung it a second time. It tore the tool from her hands, jerking her forward so she tumbled face down on the ice.

The Spider's other arm shot out and grabbed Peters around the bicep.

Peters screamed, dropping the camera, and the bug scuttled backwards, dragging him away into the storm.

OUTPOST ZERO, ANTARCTICA
21 HOURS AGO

Sofia lay on the ice watching the shadow fade from black to grey. When it was gone, she stared at the emptiness of the swirling blizzard.

Another person, in the same situation, might have despaired. They might have given up. They might have decided it was easier to stay where they were and wait for the Spider to return for them. What else could they do?

The thought crossed her mind, but no, Sofia Diaz was not the kind of girl who gave up. She did not lie back and accept what was happening to her. Sofia had been in difficult situations before. She enjoyed danger, she loved the thrill of adventure, and she liked to be in control.

As a Scout, Sofia had learnt the meaning of 'Be Prepared'. She had printed it out on a piece of paper and stuck it on her wall so she would never forget it. Right underneath it was another motto that had served her well when she had been rock climbing or on survival weekends in the Outback. Being prepared was great, but sometimes things go wrong. And whenever that happened, she had a back-up; the unofficial motto of the United States Marine Corps.

Improvise, adapt and overcome.

That's what she had to do now. She told herself to get a grip, sort herself out and get on her feet. There was no excuse for lying there doing nothing. Not ever. She might not know what was going on, but she was going to do everything she could to find out, and to warn anyone else who came to Outpost Zero. She would improvise, adapt and overcome.

She opened her mouth and screamed into the storm. She shouted so loud and hard that her voice was like broken glass when it ripped from her throat. It was a battle cry, tearing out of her; her promise to the storm that she was going to fight.

She scrambled to her feet and pulled the tracker from her pocket. A blue dot – all that was left of Peters – was travelling away from her at high speed, rushing across the airstrip towards Storage, but Sofia couldn't afford to waste time thinking about him; there were two other Spiders out there somewhere and she had to reach safety. She shoved the scanner back into her pocket, snatched up the camera Peters had dropped, and hurried across the landing strip, keeping the guide rope in her left hand as she ran. The tightness of the rope was reassuring. It would get her back. It would lead her to–

The rope slackened and slumped into the snow behind her. Somewhere in the storm, something had cut it.

The Spiders. They've come for me.

Forcing the panic down, Sofia kept hold of the loose rope and battled on through the storm as shadows gathered. Hidden by the weather, more monsters were moving in the darkness, cruising, testing, waiting for the right time to strike.

'Get away!' Sofia yelled at them. 'Leave me alone!' There had to be something she could do to protect herself, something that would give her time to get to The Hub.

The flare gun!

It was still in her pocket. It wasn't much, but it was better than nothing, and it might give her the time she needed – it might be the difference between life and death. Using her teeth, she pulled the glove from her right hand and flicked it away. Without the glove, she was able to move more freely, but it wouldn't be long before the cold bit into her skin and turned her fingers black. She had to be quick.

She dug the flare gun from her pocket, thumbed back the hammer, and aimed at the main cluster of shadows.

When she fired, a sharp *pop!* punctuated the wind, and sparks jumped from the barrel of the pistol as the flare shot out. It travelled no more than a few metres before hitting something hard – *ting!* – and coming to an abrupt stop. The flare bounced away and dropped into the snow, bursting into a bright dance of red sparks that illuminated the surrounding area like brake lights on a foggy motorway. In the red glow, Sofia saw the silhouettes of two Spiders identical to the one that had taken Peters, but they didn't come forward to attack her. Instead, they recoiled from the bright light of the flare, jerking away as if it had caused them pain.

It's the way they see.

The Spiders were equipped with cameras allowing them to see in different ways. That's why they had found it so easy to track her and Peters in the storm. They had heat-vision, night-vision, infra-red, microscopic. And the brightness and warmth of the flare had interfered with all of those. If she could keep them blinded, damage the camera, she might have a chance.

With her left hand hindered by her thick glove, and her right beginning to go numb, Sofia fumbled as she reloaded the gun. She cursed her clumsy fingers as she struggled to push the flare into the chamber, then snapped the gun closed and fired another shot. This time she aimed at the ground directly in front of the two Spiders. *Pop!* The flare sparked and burst into a bright flash of red. Smoke filled the air around it, creating a swirling cloud to hide her escape.

Sofia fired once more before reloading, pocketing the gun, and reaching for the guide rope. The Spiders were turning this way and that, trying to locate her, but she had stolen a few precious seconds and didn't have much further to go. She kept the loose rope in her left hand, following it until it grew taut as she came to the place where she had tied it to the Magpie.

The silhouette of The Hub filled the storm in front of her, and she knew she was almost there.

I'm going to make it.

But the Spiders were closing in. A few more seconds, and they would have her.

Sofia pushed harder than she had ever pushed before. She forced herself to keep moving. She drew on every last reserve of energy, calling on every muscle to work harder. Reaching the stairs, she grabbed the handrail to haul herself up. At the top, she ripped open the panel beside the door and yanked hard on the emergency lever. The door clunked, hissed and slid open. Sofia lunged inside as the first Spider reached the bottom step. Its legs clattered, metal against metal. She spun around, slamming her fist hard against the lock, glimpsing the Spider trying to climb the stairs as the door slid shut.

'And stay out!' She flicked the lock, sealing the door.

Sofia shook the blood back into her numb hand and, in the darkness of The Hub, fumbled her way towards the door at the back of the room. She checked the walkway was clear, and headed across as fast as she could. When she reached Refuge, she went into the office and dropped into the chair in front of the desk. It was the same chair robotics engineer Dr Adam Reeves would pull out to access ViBac less than a day later.

Sofia was out of breath when she directed the camera at herself and started recording. Her cheeks were red raw from the cold. Pushing back her hood and lifting the goggles on to her forehead, she stared into the lens.

'Somebody will find this,' she said. 'I don't know who; but *someone* will, and I'm hoping it'll help. Everything I know is here. Somehow the Spiders have . . . come to life. Sounds crazy saying it out loud but it's like they have a life of their own. There's those things on the back of everyone's necks, and . . . something in Papa's nose. Something grey, like the thing Doc Blair found in the ice core. I reckon the others will have them too, but I didn't have time to check, we just had to get out of there, me and Prof Peters . . .' Sofia looked away from the camera and wiped her nose. 'Yeah. Prof Peters is probably one of them now.' She closed her eyes and banged her closed fist against her forehead a couple of times before turning to stare at the camera. 'It's got to be something to do with those guys from BioMesa. They brought something up from The Chasm. This *has* to be something to do with them. It has to and . . .' Sofia shook her head. 'And I brought it back here. This is my fault. I did this. I'm so sorry, I . . .' She stopped. 'I'm going to fix this. I'll . . . I don't know how . . . I'll try to get the comms working, get a message out, then I'll see if I can get my head round what's going on here. Power's off and it's getting colder, I can't sit here doing nothing. Improvise, adapt and overcome. That's the way forward. That's what I'll do; head out to where they were bringing up the ice cores. There must be something there to explain all this.

Maybe . . .' She looked down as something occurred to her. 'OK. I'm going to upload this video to ViBac, and then I'm going to try comms and see what I can find out. Wish me luck.'

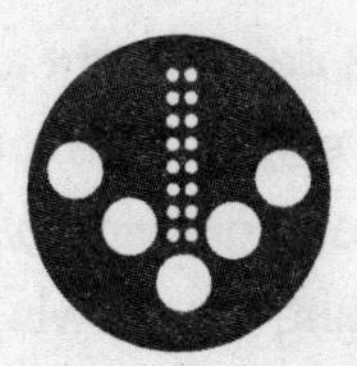

OUTPOST ZERO, ANTARCTICA
NOW

When the screen froze, Zak and the others stared at the fuzzy picture of Sofia Diaz. Zak had about twenty-five billion thoughts in his head, but the one that floated to the surface was about her. She was tough, resourceful, confident – everything he wished *he* could be – and even though he'd never met her, he knew he liked her. But they hadn't seen any sign of her since arriving at Outpost Zero.

Because they got her, Zak thought. *She didn't escape.*

She wasn't in Refuge, so those bug things must have got her and she was in Storage, right now, standing like a zombie with the others. She probably had one of those disgusting things inside her.

'They were like the things we saw in the lab,' he said.

'What's that?' May asked.

'Those bugs coming out of his clothes. And the thing in his nose. They're like what we saw in the lab. And when the Spider attacked me before, I saw stuff underneath it like . . . like something was growing there. And it looked the same as that grey thing.'

'Growing?' May pulled a face. 'On the Spider?'

'Yeah.' And the more Zak thought about it, the more positive he was that those sinews hadn't been growing *into* the main body, they had been growing *out* of it.

'How could something be growing on it?' Mum asked. 'What could be *growing* on it?'

'It's those insect things,' Zak said. 'The things they brought out of the ice.'

'Zak . . .' Mum gave him one of those sympathetic looks, but there was something else beneath the expression. Her mouth tightened and the zigzag scar under her nose had gone white. It looked to Zak a lot like fear. 'There has to be a rational explanation for this.' She put a hand on his shoulder. 'There *has* to be.'

'It's those things; I know you can see that. You don't have to pretend you're not scared. You saw them coming out of his clothes. One of them was *inside* him, we all saw it. Those people are being controlled and it's got something to do with those insects. And if they can control a person, why not everything else? The whole base. The communications and–'

'Insects controlling people?' Dad took off his glasses. 'That's . . . no, this has to be something else.'

But as he said it, they heard a sound from out on the walkway.

Tick-tack-tick-tack.

They froze.

Tick-tack-tick-tack.

When it stopped, all they could hear was the faint bluster of the dying storm.

'I think they've come for us,' Zak said.

'No.' May pushed back against the desk. 'It's the girl from the video. Or the others have woken up and now they're all right.'

'Sh.' Dad pushed in front of them. He engaged the lock and put his face close to the window in the office door.

'D'you see anything?' Zak asked.

'Sh.' Dad raised a finger to his lips.

'I don't want to be like them. Like the people on the video.' May spoke quickly and quietly. 'I don't want those things on me.'

'You won't get anything on you,' Mum said. 'Dad and I won't let that happen.' She moved to stand in front of her.

May peered at Zak through strands of black hair. 'I won't be like them.' A cold strength settled in her expression. 'I *won't*.'

Zak's mind was a jumble of all the crazy things that had happened over the last few hours. He felt like he had slipped out of his body and was watching from somewhere far away.

'And I won't let them get *you* either,' May said. 'I promise.' She clamped her jaw tight, and Zak saw a determination in her eyes he had never seen before, and for some weird reason it actually made him feel more secure.

'It's all right,' Dad whispered. 'The door's locked. That thing's not getting in here.'

'Thing?' Mum asked. 'What *thing*?'

One by one, Zak and Mum and May crept towards the door and peered out. What Zak saw filled his veins with ice.

A smaller, cruder version of the Spiders was standing in the doorway to Refuge. About the size of a large, heavy dog, the main bulk of its dark metal body was raised a few centimetres off the ground; its legs poised either side. What could only have been a CCTV camera was mounted at the front, watching them. It didn't come into the corridor, but waited, each of its six legs tapping the ground in turn.

Tick. Tack. Tick. Tack.

One at a time.

Tick. Tack. Tick. Tack.

'What the hell is that?' Zak whispered.

'It looks like a crude imitation of the Spiders.' Mum glanced at Dad.

'Built using parts from the Magpie?' he said. 'And the plane?'

'That's what it looks like. There are composite components too,' Mum said. 'That's incredible.'

'You think *they* did that?' Dad sounded unsure. 'The Spiders? You think they took parts from the plane so they could build that . . . thing?' He shook his head. 'That's impossible.'

Impossible. Can't be. Doesn't make sense. Another explanation. Impossible, impossible, impossible. That's all Zak was hearing from Mum and Dad.

He couldn't believe they still sounded like this was all so fascinating. Yeah, the robot thing was amazing and everything, but it was dangerous. It was covered in patches of grey yucky stuff that looked *alive*, and he was sure it wanted to do awful things to them. It wanted to control their minds, turn them into zombies and . . . what? That was the worst thing. They just didn't know.

Outside, the drone thing settled back and turned its camera directly at Zak.

As it did so, he felt a deep warmth expand behind his right eye. It spread like ink in water, washing over him, pulsing and aching, exploding in a powerful jolt. A brightness erupted inside him, filling everything. His muscles tingled, his blood fizzed, and his thoughts were wiped away by a busy hail of white noise. It was as if his whole body was caught in an electrical storm. Zak was paralysed, and there was the strange sensation again, of something being inside his head, crawling over his thoughts.

Images erupted in his mind.

Bam! Zak was sitting in Mr Anderson's office – not *Doctor* Anderson because consultants prefer *Mister* – listening to why he had been getting so many headaches and why he'd had that the seizure during French. There was something growing in his brain, so the doctor was going to put Zak to sleep and drill a small hole in his head and take a sample of what was in there and . . .

Bam! Zak was wearing a pale blue hospital gown – *why is it always pale blue?* – and he was watching himself from the corner of the room as the doctor touched the drill to the side of his head and pressed the trigger and . . .

Bam! He was back in the doctor's office, Mum and Dad with serious faces as Mr Anderson explained the treatment that would follow and . . .

Bam! He was in Antarctica, staring at an old-fashioned explorer who was standing by a huge crack in the ice, beckoning to him with both hands and . . .

Bam! He was floating above a shimmering sea of insects crawling over one another, taking flight, rising in two never-ending spirals of fluorescent yellow and . . .

The images stopped. A flash of white, and the presence inside his head began to move away like a silk sheet slowly slipping away from a table to reveal the wood beneath.

Zak blinked and the drone-thing was still there in the doorway to Refuge. May was still beside him.

Whatever had just happened to Zak, no one had noticed. They had either been too busy watching the thing outside, or it had happened too quickly for them to see, but his legs felt weak and when he put a hand on May to steady himself, she turned to look at him.

'I'm . . .' Wasn't it time to tell them? About the polar bear? About the explorer? About the feeling that something was trying to get into his head? It was important. He was sure it had something to do with what was happening here. But he didn't know where to start. How could he even *begin* to tell them?

'It's moving,' Mum said. She tightened her lips and her zigzag scar went white again.

Zak looked back at the window to see the mechanical monstrosity lift itself a little higher off the ground and shift backwards.

'Is it letting us past?' Mum asked. 'Is that what it's doing?'

Before any of them could answer, a group of small spiders came into view, scuttling into the corridor like an army. At least twenty of them, they swept across the pale blue floor. They were similar in size and shape to the scuttling thing that had attacked them in the Drone Bay, and the things they'd seen attached to the people in Storage, but these were different. They had evolved.

As they advanced into Refuge, the lock on the office door disengaged with a quiet click, and the door slid open.

JANUARY ISLAND, SOUTH CHINA SEA
2 HOURS AGO

'Why don't you come in, Dad?'

The Broker glanced up from the smartphone and watched his eldest son drag himself out of the pool, dripping on the expensive Italian tiles. Even this early, when the sun had barely risen, his children loved to be in the water.

'Come on, don't be so boring.'

Putting the smartphone on the glass-topped table, he shook his head. 'You know me, David. I prefer to stay dry. Anyway, I've just had my breakfast.' He indicated the lavish spread of fresh fruit and pastries on the poolside table in front of him – Chef always put out far too much and The Broker sometimes wondered if she was trying to make him fat. Or *fatter*. 'And you know what they say about swimming too soon after you've eaten.'

'That's a myth.' David smiled and flicked water across his father's face. 'Wimp.'

'Careful.' The Broker gave his son a fake stern look. 'This is the shirt your mother gave me for our anniversary.'

'And you'd better not ruin it.' Sitting beside him, his wife, Natalia, spoke without taking her eyes off her *Town and Country* magazine. 'That cost a fortune.'

David ignored her and flicked water at his dad again, spraying a line of dark spots across the deep red silk shirt.

'Stop it. She'll kill me if it gets ruined.' The Broker cast a sly glance at his wife, pretending to be worried, but when David came closer, he cracked a smile that showed perfect white teeth. 'Cheeky monkey.' He leapt from his seat at the table and gave chase as his son made a quick getaway. 'I'll get you for that.'

The boy darted across the tiles and on to the well-tended grass. He dodged this way and that, but the Broker was quick despite his size. When the boy feinted left for the third time, The Broker caught his wrist in one powerful hand and pulled the boy towards him.

'Now for your punishment!' He bent at the knees and took his son's leg in his other hand, hoisting him over his head. He strode towards the pool, went right to the edge, and threw the boy as far as he could.

The boy hit the middle of the swimming pool with a huge splash that sent waves filtering out in all directions.

'I am invincible!' The Broker raised his arms above his head and fist-pumped the air. 'No one can–'

'That's what you think.' His daughter had crept up behind him, ready to shove her father into the pool. But The Broker's instincts were keen. Before she could put her hands on him, he twisted, snatched her arms towards him, and threw her in beside her brother.

'It'll take more than that to sneak up on *me*, young lady.'

'How do you do that?' she laughed. 'How did you know?'

'I'm always watching, Jennifer.' He touched two fingers to his eyes, then pointed at her. 'I see everything, remember.'

'Next time.' She splashed water at him. 'I'll get you, next time.'

The Broker stepped back to avoid being drenched, and stood admiring his children as they dived beneath the surface. He had so much to be grateful for. His wealth, his health, his family.

A faint *ping* interrupted his thoughts and he glanced back at the breakfast table. His wife peered over the top of her magazine and lowered her sunglasses. 'No rest for the wicked, darling.'

'No rest indeed,' he said, returning to the table and sitting down to check the large smartphone. The name '**Phoenix**' was displayed on the screen.

The Broker poured himself another pineapple juice, and picked up the phone.

'I have an update for you, sir.'

'I'm in a good mood, Phoenix. Please don't spoil it.' The Broker smiled to his wife. In turn, she reached across and rubbed the back of his hand.

'Lazarovich is almost on site, sir. Everything is going according to schedule.'

'Perfect.'

'There is one, thing, though.'

The Broker narrowed his eyes and his smile dropped away. 'Go on.'

'If you take a look at the image I've sent through.'

'Just a moment.' The Broker took the phone from his ear. He clicked the icon that appeared, and the screen filled with a satellite image of the base. It was similar to the previous images, except for one or two things. One of those things was the small plane on the landing strip. He double-tapped it to zoom in for a better view and studied the image for a few seconds. When he was ready, he put the phone back to his ear. 'Explain.'

'It's a Twin Otter, sir, flown in from the South Shetland Islands. The pilot goes by the name of Dimitri Alekseyevich Milanov. Records show he's a failed military pilot. He's of no concern to us. The plane was carrying four passengers, though – Drs Evelyn and Adam Reeves, and their two children, Zak and May.'

'Shame.'

'How do you wish us to proceed, sir?'

The Broker exchanged a glance with his wife, and then fixed his eyes on the pool where his children were still playing. He thought about the plane on the landing strip, and the five people it had contained. Drs Evelyn and Adam Reeves might be a valuable asset to his organization if he could find a way of arranging it so they didn't know they were working for him – he had no interest in *forcing* them to work for him. Or, perhaps, he could sell them. But that was not the aim of this mission. The aim was to find out what BioMesa had discovered beneath the ice, and take control of it. The more he thought about it, the more convinced he was that they had found something of huge importance. Something of great value.

The Broker's daughter burst from the surface of the pool and shook the water from her eyes, before raising a hand and waving. He returned the wave, feeling a surge of love for his children, then looked once more at the image on his smartphone. The plane on the runway.

No, the Reeves family was an unnecessary distraction.

He stood and walked a few paces away from the table. 'Eliminate them,' he said. 'No one can know about this.'

'All of them, sir?'

'Yes. All of them.' The Broker ended the call with a quick tap of his thumb, and returned to sit beside his wife. He leant over and kissed her on the cheek.

'Work trouble?' Natalia lowered her magazine and watched her husband.

'In a manner of speaking.'

'Nothing you can't handle, I'm sure. Just don't let it ruin your mood.'

The Broker smiled in agreement. 'I won't, Natalia. I

promise. Everything will turn out fine.' He kissed her again, then sat back and closed his eyes.

The sun was warm on his face.

It was going to be a glorious day.

OUTPOST ZERO, ANTARCTICA
NOW

Tick-tack-tick-tack. Zak's ears were filled with the scary scurrying sound of tiny legs tapping against the solid floor. Any second now, they would be inside.

Dad went straight for the controls, slamming his fist on the button. 'Close!' he shouted as he pummelled at it. 'Close!' But the door remained open.

Tick-tack-tick-tack.

'Manual override!' Mum moved forward to join Dad, but he yelled at her to get back.

'Stay with the kids!'

Mum retreated to stand in front of Zak and May,

stretching her arms out like it would do any good. Dad fumbled with the panel to the override lever. In his panic, he struggled to get his fingers into the gap.

'They're coming!' May shouted.

'I know!' Dad abandoned his attempts with the door and stepped back to face the invading creatures as they came into view.

The scuttling spider-things had patches of shining black armour on their backs, grey and fleshy joints, and legs edged with hard serrations. They were a mechanical skeleton with an organic – *living* – covering, but they looked as if they hadn't yet finished becoming what they were supposed to be. They hadn't finished *growing*.

They moved fast, reaching the door in seconds, and Dad stamped hard on the first to enter the room.

Bullseye. There was a crunch and a squish as the bug crushed beneath the tread of his boot.

His success gave Zak a sudden burst of hope, but when Dad raised his foot again, bringing it down hard, the second spider-thing leapt aside at the last moment, and he stamped on nothing but air and pale blue flooring. Unbalanced by his failure, Dad faltered, and the thing took advantage of his vulnerability. It jumped on to the top of his boot and darted upwards, its serrated legs clinging to the material of his trousers. Dad whirled around, stamping his foot, flailing to brush the monster away. As he struggled, another bug sprang on to his boot and began working its way up.

With a gasp, Mum rushed forward, beating her hands at

Dad as if she were trying to put out a fire. 'Get off him! Get off!'

More of the miniature monsters scuttled around them, and Mum took a couple out purely by accident, crunching them with the grim sound of cracking and squelching. But there were too many of them. They latched on to her boots and began racing up her legs. Others continued deeper into the room, heading straight for Zak and May.

'No!' May surged into action. 'This is not happening!' She dashed to the side of the room where a fire extinguisher was clipped to the wall. She tugged it from its fixings and pulled out the nozzle, turning to point it at the floor. Without hesitation, she squeezed the handle and *WHOOSH!* a burst of carbon dioxide shot from the extinguisher and engulfed the bugs in a billowing white cloud.

Small as they were, a direct hit from the extinguisher sent the scuttlers spinning away into the corridor. For a few seconds, they were disorientated, and May rushed forward to fire the extinguisher at Mum and Dad who were trying to swat the things from their clothes. With a *WHOOOOSH!* they disappeared in a huge cloud, and Zak heard the sound of the spider-things dropping to the floor.

As soon as she had done it, May raised the fire extinguisher and brought it down on the nearest monster, killing it with a sickening crunch.

By the door, the rest of them were beginning to recover and regroup. They were moving again, turning this way and that in confusion, their legs skittering on the floor.

Zak spun around, searching for a weapon, desperate

to help.

What would Jackson Jones do? And then he had an idea.

'May!' Zak grabbed the Ranged Chemical Delivery System from the wall and held it like a rifle. 'They're coming back!' He pointed it at the bugs and pulled the trigger and–

– nothing happened. He tried the trigger again, squeezing it four or five times in quick succession, but still nothing happened.

'The red button!' Dad shouted. 'By the handle!'

Zak pushed the button and aimed the Ranger once more, pointing it at the creatures that were making their way back into the room.

'You have to pump the slide,' Dad yelled at him. 'The part in your left hand.'

Zak knew exactly what he meant – it was just like the Nerf gun he had at home – so he racked the slide once, took aim and fired. This time there was a loud *POP!* and a fraction of a second later, a cloud of grey powder exploded on the ground by the door. It sprayed outwards like a burst bag of flour, instantly becoming a thick, cloudy gas that billowed out, obscuring the door. It lasted only a few seconds before it thinned and disappeared but, once again, the bugs were stunned by the attack.

'Quick! Before they try again!' He rushed forward, stamping his feet, and the others joined him like it was some kind of weird dance. The spider-things died under their boots with such a satisfying crunch that Zak was filled with a sense of power – of actually *doing* something. 'In your face, bugs!' he shouted as he stamped on another. 'In. Your.

FACE!' The bug popped like a fat blueberry.

Gas drifted around him like smoke on a battlefield. The hard remains of bug shells and mechanical parts lay like broken machines of war. Sticky pools of disgusting grey mush were splattered around the floor. And Zak continued to stamp at the scuttlers. To stamp them out of existence. To kill, kill, kill.

'I think that's enough now.' May touched his arm. 'You can stop.'

Zak scanned the room. 'Did we get them all?' His blood was up, his adrenaline raging. 'Are they all dead?' He was out of breath, and sweating inside his coat. 'Is that all of them?'

'I think so.' May stepped back, holding the fire extinguisher like a weapon.

'That was quick thinking,' Mum said. 'Well done, you two. Are you all right?'

'Yeah.' May nudged Zak. '"*In your face*"?'

Zak grinned.

'What are they?' Mum was staring at the mess on the floor. 'They were *alive*.'

'I told you,' Zak said. 'It's something to do with those insects. This grey stuff is the same. It's like it's adding to them, or something. Growing on them. It's making them alive, and–'

'It's not over yet,' Dad said. 'That big one is still by the entrance. We need to shut it down.'

'How?' Mum asked.

'Maybe this'll work.' Zak gave May the Ranger, and

grabbed the fire extinguisher from her hands.

He strode out of the room and along the short corridor.

'Zak? Zak!?' Mum called after him, but he didn't answer; he kept on going. Didn't even flinch when Mum called his name. He marched right up to the thing that was cobbled together out of parts from the Magpie and the plane.

As he approached, he saw more of the grey stuff in its joints. Threads of it snaked back towards its brain, but he didn't care. And the strange thing was, it didn't look as if the spider-thing cared either. It just sat there, and as Zak came closer to it, he fired the extinguisher in front of him.

WHOOSH!

A cloud of carbon dioxide shot out, filling the doorway and spilling into the cold Antarctic air. For a second the spider-thing was invisible, but Zak didn't hesitate. He continued forward, picking up his pace, and turned the extinguisher in his hands so it was a solid steel battering ram. He stepped out on to the walkway and slammed it into the creature's camera.

With a noise like two cars colliding at speed, the base of the extinguisher smashed into the thing's lens, crushing glass and bending metal. The living machine shuddered under the force of the blow, moving its legs back to brace itself when Zak hit it a second time. Again came the sound of metal against metal, and the thing staggered backwards, its front legs faltering at the complicated joints. But Zak didn't stop there. He forced it to retreat further and further along the walkway, raising the extinguisher again and again, denting metal, crushing glass, and cracking the weird beetle-like armour as he broke through to its fleshy, electronic brain. And each time he hammered it, the creature staggered back a little further, its legs weakening as Zak beat it into submission.

Halfway along the metal walkway, the monster's front end tipped forward under the onslaught, its back legs skittering, trying to keep its body upright. And with a final killer blow, Zak raised the fire extinguisher high above his head like a pile driver and smashed it into the monster as hard as he could.

Pieces exploded in all directions, scattering across the walkway and shooting over the edge to fall to the ice below. The monster collapsed on to what was left of its face, then the back legs gave up, and the whole thing came crashing down like a piece of useless junk.

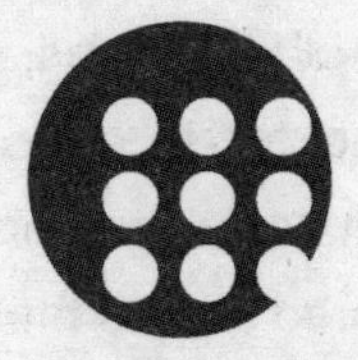

OUTPOST ZERO, ANTARCTICA
NOW

'What on earth were you thinking?' Mum called as she and the others ran to where Zak was standing.

Zak had been so worked up, so *crazed*, he hadn't realized how far out he'd come. Now that he turned to see them rushing towards him, he realized he was halfway along the walkway. The wind was whistling around him, snatching away his cloudy breath.

'What were you thinking?' Mum said again as she threw her arms around him. 'You could have been–' She stopped, but Zak knew what she had been about to say.

Killed. You could have been killed.

'You went completely nuts,' May said. 'I mean, brilliant, but bonkers.'

Zak grinned at her, adrenaline still firing through his body. He was on a high now, feeling strong. On top of the world. He felt as if he could take on a whole army of those things. Just him and his fire extinguisher.

'Don't run off like that again,' Dad told him. 'I think you're starting to enjoy this a bit too much.'

'Someone had to do something,' Zak said.

'Yeah, well.' Dad shook his head. 'It should have been me.'

'I was fine. Look what I did.' He pointed to the smashed-up Frankenstein's monster lying at his feet. There were bits and pieces of it scattered across the walkway.

'I guess we know what happened to the plane,' May said.

'How many *more* of them d'you think there are?' Mum asked.

'We need to check the other back-up files.' Dad turned towards Refuge. 'Maybe find out what happened to Sofia, see if there's anything about BioMesa. We need to find a way to stop this.'

Mum followed Dad back to Refuge, but Zak and May stayed where they were, fixated on the dead monster.

'I really kicked its butt, didn't I?' Zak said.

'Hey, don't get cocky. The fire extinguisher was my idea.'

'True,' Zak admitted. 'You were totally owning those creepy little things.'

'I just imagined it was Vanessa and her clones.'

Zak looked up at her. 'You really hate her.'

'Hate's a strong word,' May said. 'But don't forget, we're talking about the girl who posted that picture of me all over social media. The one where I was dressed as Angelina Ballerina when I was, like, five or something.'

'Good point.'

'You did good, though, little bro.' May punched his arm. 'Come on.' She shivered. 'Let's get inside.' But when she turned to head back to Refuge, she stopped and reached out to grab Zak's arm.

'What?' Startled, he spun around and immediately saw what was wrong.

There were two people inside Refuge, heading along the corridor towards the office – but it wasn't Mum and Dad. From their build, Zak thought they were both women, and they were wearing the same red jackets he had seen the settlers wearing in Sofia's video. They must have climbed up the stairs from the ice, without anyone noticing.

Zak looked at May, and she looked at him. She opened her mouth but didn't say anything. The two of them stared at each other for several long seconds before May managed to get her words out. 'Mum and Dad.'

And that broke the spell.

Zak dropped the fire extinguisher and they started to run, clomping along the walkway.

'Hey!' Zak shouted. 'Mum! Dad!'

They raced towards the two figures in red jackets.

'Behind you!' May yelled.

When Zak and May were level with the steps descending to the ice on the right, the red-jackets reached the office.

A few paces closer, and the door slipped open.

By the time Zak and May reached the entrance to Refuge, the figures had entered the office and the door had closed behind them.

'Mum! Dad!' Zak's voice was ragged from shouting. He thumped along the short corridor and slammed into the office door. He punched the button, but the door remained shut.

'No! No, no, no, no!' Zak hammered at the door opener.

May banged her fists against the window.

'No!' Zak fumbled to pull open the emergency manual release, but still the door remained shut. All he could do now was watch helplessly through the window at the horror unfolding inside.

Sofia's mama and papa were inside the office, along with her brother, Pablo, and another one of the red-jacketed zombies. Crammed into the small space, two of them had grabbed Dad. They were holding him tight, as if they were hugging him. Or trying to squeeze him to death. Another two were doing the same to Mum. Both Mum and Dad were struggling, trying to move and shake them off, but the red-jackets were too strong.

'Stop!' May was shouting. 'Please!'

Zak yanked the emergency lever again and banged on the release button, but nothing worked. Giving up, he joined May, hammering on the window, but the red-jackets were not distracted from their task.

'Break it,' May shouted at Zak. 'We need to break it!'

Zak grabbed the fire extinguisher from beside the

entrance. He turned it endways on and smashed it as hard as he could against the window – *THUD!* The reinforced glass was too strong, and the fire extinguisher bounced back, hitting him in the face.

'Give it to me!' May told him.

THUD! This time Zak was ready for the impact but still the window wouldn't break.

Inside, the red-jackets held on to Mum and Dad as insects began to emerge from their cuffs. Black and shining, the first ones scuttled out from Pablo's sleeve and ran across his hand.

Zak hit the window again.

Insects crawled out from the neckline of their jackets, from beneath the hems, pouring over their bodies, covering their arms, turning them black.

THUD!

The bugs scurried over Mum and Dad's shoulders, rushing up their necks and smothering their faces.

THUD!

More and more of them poured out from inside the red-jackets' clothes. Some of them took to the air, shimmering in a translucent dance, swirling together, moving in the same way Zak had seen inside the lab. Like he had seen in his vision. And after a few seconds, some of them displayed fluorescent yellow spots and began to move faster and faster, creating a hypnotic double spiral pattern.

THUD!

'What are they doing?' May shouted. 'What's happening?'

The bugs on Dad's face began to shed their hard casings,

the armour falling away to reveal the ugly translucent things inside. Narrow, soft and segmented, with too many legs, and an earwig-like pincer at the end of their bodies.

The same was happening to Mum. The insects crawling over her mouth and nose began to emerge from their armour. Mum and Dad were shaking their heads, fighting against the red-jackets, but neither of them could break away, neither of them could dislodge the creatures clinging to their bodies.

Zak was filled with horror and revulsion when he saw one of the soft insects try to push into Dad's mouth. Dad bit down, cutting it in half with a splurge of goo, but when he tried to spit it out, another slipped between his lips and disappeared beneath his tongue. Beside him, one of the monsters extended its segmented tail into Mum's nostril, the pincer-like tip feeling its way into her nose. It latched on and constricted, pulling itself inside.

Smash! The window gave in, shattering tiny fragments into the office and letting out a blast of warm air, but Zak was too late.

The red-jackets released Mum and Dad, leaving them both standing bolt upright, arms by their sides. Their eyes were wide, their chests heaving with fear and exhaustion as the remaining armourless insects pushed into their mouths, disappearing from view.

The rest of the insects spread their wings and joined the others in that hypnotic, spiral dance.

Dad tried to speak. His mouth opened and closed, like a fish out of water, gasping for life. His eyes bulged, his body trembled and . . . he stopped. His eyes softened and he stared ahead, his face blank. His breathing slowed to a steady beat, and his jaw slackened. 'Join us.'

'Oh no.' May stepped back. 'No. Please. No.'

Mum's breathing returned to normal. Her expression relaxed and her eyes glazed over. 'Join us.'

Zak couldn't move. His mind was swirling. His muscles were numb.

'Join us.'

'Stop saying that!' May screamed.

The black cloud of insects buzzed and clattered and flickered with colour. It spun in the air inside the office, gathering itself together, shifting direction and swarming towards the broken window.

Zak's thoughts darkened. An ache pulsed deep inside his head, beating in time with his heart. The world around him began to disappear and he saw faded images in his mind. He saw a sea of writhing insects begin to form. He saw ancient explorers on the ice, beckoning to him. He saw mountains and forests and creatures crawling from boiling seas.

The feeling in his legs began to slip away, his body becoming weightless and–

May wrenched the fire extinguisher from his grip, her sudden movement breaking the spell that held Zak in place. Without even thinking, he moved out of her way as May lifted the nozzle of the fire extinguisher and pointed it at the jagged hole in the reinforced glass. She stepped back and squeezed the handle.

As the insects streamed out into the corridor, May hit them with a long jet of carbon dioxide. The force of it was strong enough to break up the swarm, scattering bugs everywhere. They pitter-pattered like hard rain as they spun away into the walls and fell to the floor.

May didn't stop until the extinguisher was empty and the corridor was filled with a fog of carbon dioxide. The white cloud surrounded them, but it quickly dissipated into the cold air, revealing the insects on the pale blue floor – some crawling in a daze, others on their backs, struggling to turn over. Zak crushed two under his boot, but before he could do it again, May dropped the spent fire extinguisher and grabbed him by the arm, trying to pull him away.

'No, wait.' He pushed her off. 'We have to kill them.'

'There's too many,' May told him. 'And look.'

Zak glanced into the office and saw the red-jackets advancing towards the door. Mum and Dad had joined them, blank-faced and terrifying.

On the floor, the insects were recovering, opening their wings and buzzing like wasps as they began to take to the air once more.

'We have to *run*,' May shouted. 'Now!'

OUTPOST ZERO, ANTARCTICA
NOW

So they ran.

There was nothing else for them to do.

Zak and May left Mum and Dad behind, and they ran for their lives. With insects filling the air behind them like a diseased cloud, Zak and May retreated through Refuge and burst out on to the walkway. It was difficult to run in heavy boots and layers of clothing, but they were fuelled by the terror of what would happen to them if they stayed still. The thought of those insects crawling on them, working their way inside them.

The clatter of wings was drowned by the sound of their

boots on the metal walkway, but Zak knew the insects were there. He knew they wouldn't stop until everybody at Outpost Zero was . . . what? Infected? Controlled? He had no idea what the insects were trying to do, but he was sure of one thing: if he ended up like the red-jackets – like *Mum and Dad* – there would be no one to help. There would be no one to put this right. So Zak pushed himself as hard as he could, trying to keep up with May. But as they came close to the end of the walkway, the door to The Hub slid open and light spilt out towards them.

May came to a stop, her boots skidding on the icy metal, and Zak collided into her, getting a faceful of his sister's coat. The two of them stumbled forwards, grabbing the railing for support, startled by the red-jackets waiting for them inside The Hub. Zak reckoned there must have been at least ten of them standing there, all with their hands out, insects crawling over their arms and necks.

'Why won't you leave us alone!' May screamed as the red-jackets stepped out of The Hub and into the cold.

Zak's first reaction was to run the other way, but when he turned round, he saw Mum and Dad, and the others advancing towards them, insects swirling above their heads in a cloud.

'We're trapped,' Zak said.

'I'm not going to end up like them.'

Zak scanned in both directions along the walkway, then leant over the handrail beside him. 'Only one way out of this.' The ground was about five metres below and looked like a bed of snow.

'Over there?' May said. 'You're serious?'

'You got a better idea?'

'I guess not.' May pulled up on to the railing and swung her legs over. Zak climbed up beside her.

They sat on the railing with their legs dangling over the long drop to the ice below.

'You ready?' May asked.

'No.' Zak forced a smile. 'Definitely not.' Then he pushed himself off.

The fall was brief. There was just a moment of weightlessness before Zak hit the ground. He had expected it to be soft, but he was wrong. The wind had blown some of the snow into shallow drifts around the walkway supports, and Zak was lucky enough to land in one of those, but it wasn't much more than a few centimetres deep. As soon as he touched down, he bent his knees to absorb the impact, letting his energy take him forwards into a roll. But what he thought would be cat-like and agile, actually turned into a face plant. His legs crumpled, his arms folded beneath him and he slammed forward into the shallow drift.

A second later, May came down with a thump and collapsed on top of him, knocking the air out of his lungs. '*Oof.*'

As soon as he regained his breath, Zak pushed his sister off and got to his feet. He held out a hand to help her up. 'You OK?'

'I think so.'

His knees ached from the landing, and his ankle was hurting from a mild twist, but he had other concerns. Above them, the sound of boots on the metal walkway had stopped. Zak stood back and craned his neck to see the underside of the punched metal, the dark shapes of the red-jackets.

'What now?' May said. 'Where do we go now?'

'Hub.' He turned to his sister. 'Yeah. The Hub. We'll go underneath, then in through the front.'

Zak glanced up at the walkway one more time, and began trudging across the snow as quickly as he could. May hurried alongside him as they headed towards the struts supporting The Hub. To their right, the Drone Bay skulked like a shadowy presence, and Zak half expected the lift to whir into action, but it remained silent.

'Are they following?' May looked over her shoulder.

'I don't think so.' Zak picked up his pace, pushing himself harder. The thought of those zombie people out there, hiding in the shadows, filled him with terror. He and May had to find somewhere safe and warm. Somewhere to hide. Somewhere to defend themselves.

But as he grabbed May's coat sleeve, encouraging her to hurry, he heard a steady rhythm beating on the ice. A Spider.

Tick-tack-tick-tack. Tick-tack-tick-tack.

'Oh my God, it's coming!' May's voice was tight and high. 'It's coming!'

They thought they were already moving as quickly as they could, but when they heard the sound behind them, they found something extra. They pushed themselves harder and fixed their eyes on the nearest corner of The Hub.

The sub-zero air hurt Zak's lungs with every breath he sucked in.

Almost there.

The Spider was gaining on them.

Tick-tack-tick-tack.

It was so close now. Zak could hear its metal parts working; the hydraulics pumping in and out, the joints clicking and clacking.

Keep going.

Ahead, a thick steel strut rose from the ice, supporting The Hub a couple of metres above the ground. All Zak had to do was get to it. Not much further and he would be safe for a while at least. The Spider would be too big to follow them under there.

Usually, Zak laughed at May's peculiar, legs-out-to-the-side running style, and she laughed along with him, exaggerating it when they played on the field near their house. But right now, the unusual running style was helping her. Instead of having to drag her boots through the snow, she was clearing it with every step, and she managed to forge a few paces in front of Zak. When she reached The Hub, she threw her legs out in front of her and skidded to safety.

May picked herself up and turned to watch Zak approach. 'Run!' she screamed at him. 'Run!' She waved her hands, beckoning as if it might somehow make him run faster.

But Zak didn't need May to tell him. He could feel the Spider coming closer and closer. The ground was shaking beneath him; the sound of its clicks and whirrs were echoing in his ears. He felt the warmth of its batteries and the approaching darkness of another vision just before he planted both feet on the ground and pushed off with as much force as he could muster.

Zak put out his hands and dived under The Hub. He landed in the snow and skidded to a halt beside his sister. Behind him, there was a heavy thud as the Spider collided with the lowest edge of building, and the dark vision that had threatened to suffocate Zak disappeared. He sat up to see the machine reeling as it tried to maintain its balance.

In the light from the now clear sky, he could see the muscle and sinew glistening on the underside of the Spider.

'We have to keep going.' Zak took May's hand and they helped each other to their feet. 'I'm not waiting for that thing to come to its senses.'

They left the Spider reeling from its collision, and hurried along beneath The Hub, heading towards the front where it faced the airstrip. When Zak had been inside the building, it hadn't felt so big, but now he was outside, and in a hurry, it seemed enormous. Zak felt as if he was in a bad dream, running towards something that never gets any closer.

Halfway across, Zak heard a thump and glanced back to see the Spider scurrying over the ice behind the Hub. It was too big to crawl beneath the buildings, and had to make its way around the entire base, but it was still desperate to catch its prey. It moved quickly, so close to the back of the Hub that it banged against it with every third or fourth step, skittering and slipping as it changed direction to stumble past the Science labs. But it wouldn't be fast enough. Zak and May would reach the front before it completely regained its senses and caught them.

'What if we can't get inside?' Zak panted.

'What? Why would . . ? What do you mean?'

'They can control the doors; they'll stop us from getting in.'

'No.' May slowed down. 'No way.'

'Or they'll be waiting for us, like before.'

'They won't be. We'll get inside and find a place to hide and . . . just come on.' She grabbed him and pulled him with her, dragging him the final few metres to the edge of The Hub and out into the open.

May didn't waste any time. As soon as they emerged from beneath the building she hurried to the steps and climbed to the front entrance. Zak was right on her heels as she pulled the emergency lever and the door swished open.

The light and the blast of warm air were a welcome relief that lasted less than a second. In an instant, Zak caught a snapshot of the interior of the base, and put out a hand to stop May who was about to blunder inside.

At least fifteen of the red-jackets were standing by the spiral staircase. They were in a line, facing the entrance, eyes closed. As soon as the door opened, their eyes flicked open to stare at the two intruders.

'Join us.'

The room was different from the way Zak had seen it

before. Instead of being pale blue, the floor was now covered with large patches of shining black insects. They were on the furniture, on the walls, smothering the kitchen, covering the staircase. The smell coming from The Hub was musty and rank.

Almost immediately, the insects rose into the air as one – as if a silent communication had passed among them – and they began to twist and flicker in the light.

Zak pulled May back, and together they tumbled down the steps on to the ice.

Whatever those things were, they were overrunning the base.

They scrambled to their feet and sprinted into the night, heading away from The Hub. Zak could only think of one other place where they might be able to hide. 'The plane!' he shouted. 'Head for the plane!'

So they tore across the open ice, terrified, running for their lives.

Zak didn't look back. He didn't dare. Instead, he concentrated on the shape of the wrecked plane on the dark airstrip. If they could reach it without being seen, they had a chance.

But, as if something had read his mind, the strip lights flared into life along the length of the runway. All at once, the powerful beams shone into the clear sky, glaring in Zak's vision. Now it felt as if he and May were running towards a wall of bright light, but once they broke through it, the plane was within reach.

They raced past the bent door lying beside the discarded

pilot's chair, and hurried to the place where the cockpit was torn open. They clambered inside and scrambled along the metal floor, keeping out of sight.

When they reached the place where Zak had been sitting during their flight to Outpost Zero, he stopped and risked a peek out the window.

The Spider that was chasing them had now made it right around the base to the front of the Hub, where a black cloud of insects was pouring from the open door. They spun and twisted as if they were one creature, and as they moved, fluorescent yellow spirals flickered in the centre of the swarm.

'They're coming,' May said. 'They know we're here.'

Zak watched them with horror, and the events of the past few hours burned through his head at a thousand miles an hour. There was something he had missed. Something important. Something that–

And then it came to him. As crazy as it sounded, it suddenly made sense. 'They know what I'm thinking,' he whispered.

'What?'

Zak kept his eyes on the swirling mass. 'When we first came here, and the lights were off, I was sitting right here, in this exact seat, wishing the lights would come back on . . . and they did.'

'We were all wishing for that.'

'But later, in the base, when we needed the power to come back on, the same thing happened. And just now, when I was thinking about coming to the plane, the lights came on, like they *knew*.'

By The Hub, the Spider stood beside a swirling mass that was growing more and more agitated. The bugs were probing out into the cold, moving one way then another. And as Zak watched, a group of red-jackets passed through them, coming down the steps and standing on the ice.

'It's a coincidence,' May said.

But the red-jackets were coming in this direction, and Zak was more and more convinced there was something to it. They knew he was here. 'I've been seeing things too. And it's not my imagination. It's real. It's like something's trying to get into my head. To tell me something . . . and . . . I think it's the bugs. The visions are stronger when they're close.'

'The bugs, Zak? The bugs are talking to you?'

'Not talking. They're . . . look, I know it sounds crazy, but don't some bugs have, like, a hive mind or something?'

'A hive mind?'

'Yeah, like one big mind made up of loads of smaller minds. Like a swarm of bees working together. They move at the same time, all go in the same direction . . . they all know what the others are going to do. You know – a *hive*.'

'I know what a hive mind is, Zak. But bees use smells and funky little dances. They're not actually–'

'OK, so maybe these bugs do it in a different way. They use their *minds* to join together or . . . I don't know, but we've seen what they do. They're *smart*. So maybe they got into my head and now they know what I'm thinking . . .' He shuddered. 'Maybe I've got one inside me right now.'

'If you had one inside you, you'd be like *them*.' May looked at the red-jackets approaching across the ice. 'And you're not a bug, Zak, so why would they try to communicate with *you*?'

'I've thought about that.' He raised a hand to the side of his head. 'Maybe it's because I'm different. My brain is different. It's sick.'

'Oh, Zak.' May shook her head.

'Don't look at me like that. I'm not making this up. It really feels like–' He looked at the red-jackets advancing towards the plane, surrounded by a swarm of insects, and he had an idea. Maybe there was only one way to find out for sure. So he closed his eyes and emptied his mind. He pushed away his fear, and pictured himself and May in Refuge. It wasn't difficult; they'd been there a few minutes ago. He was careful not to think about what had happened there, and instead imagined him and May going into the office. He imagined they were tired from running, feeling clever for having outsmarted the red-jackets. They went into the office and locked the door, ducking out of sight in the shadows.

'They're going away,' May said.

Zak kept concentrating on the image. Him and May in the office. Safe. Warm.

'They're leaving.' May nudged Zak and he opened his eyes.

It was difficult to keep hold of the image in his mind while he was watching from the window, but May was right. The swirling cloud of bugs was moving back inside The Hub.

Some of the red-jackets were heading back inside too, while others were making their way around the base. Zak could see the Spider that had bashed itself dizzy. It was steadier on its legs now, scurrying back the way it had come.

'Where are they going?' May asked.

'Refuge,' Zak said. 'Because that's where I just sent them.'

'What are you talking about?'

'I'm imagining us being there, so that's where they're going. It really works. They really are reading my mind.'

OUTPOST ZERO, ANTARCTICA
NOW

As it turned out, the inside of a wrecked plane wasn't a great place to hide.

The storm might have gone, but a biting wind still found its way into the metal fuselage, moaning through the ragged tear in the front of the aircraft. It stole any body heat that escaped their ECW gear, and carried it away into the Antarctic desert. So, despite their layers of clothing and their thick coats, Zak and May shivered against the cold as they kept their faces close to the window, watching the exterior of Outpost Zero.

For now, the place was deserted. The airstrip beacons

had gone out, and the only light was that which spilt from The Hub windows.

Zak felt as if he wasn't on Earth any more. He was somewhere alien and cruel.

He shifted in the seat, moving closer to his sister. 'You OK?'

'No.'

'Me neither.' He dug in his pocket and pulled out the Snickers bar he had put there when they had been looking for food to give to Dima. Thinking back on it now, it seemed like a hundred years ago. He tore open the wrapper and offered it to May. 'If we eat something, it might help us stay warm.'

The chocolate was frozen solid and May struggled to bite off a chunk. She held it with both hands and used the teeth at the side of her mouth. Like a dog chewing a bone, she managed to bite off a chunk and start crunching.

The chocolate wasn't much, but it made things feel a little better. A little more normal. She tore off another bite and passed the Snickers to Zak. When he took it, May stood and walked deeper into the plane.

'What are you doing?'

'Dima said we had emergency camping gear.'

Zak gnawed at the chocolate and listened to May rummaging about somewhere in the semi-darkness. When she came back, she was carrying a bundle under each arm.

She dropped the bundles at Zak's feet. 'Sleeping bags. They're probably a bit stinky, but they should keep us warm. She went back towards the tail of the plane and returned with a holdall stuffed with gear. 'We might need these too.'

She opened the bag and took out a mean-looking claw hammer. She weighed it in one hand, then put it on the floor and dug into the holdall again. She pulled out an ice axe, a short-handled shovel, and a waterproof bag filled with red tubes that looked like sticks of dynamite from a cartoon.

'Flares,' May said.

They each stuffed as many flares as they could into their pockets.

'You want this?' May picked up the hammer.

Zak shook his head. 'You keep it.' He took the ice axe and turned it over in his hands. It felt weighty and deadly, like he could definitely use it to protect himself. But could he sink that serrated point into a person to defend himself? Into Mum or Dad?

He put it on the floor and grabbed the shovel. 'I'll have this.'

They unrolled the sleeping bags and put them over their legs as they sat side by side. They didn't dare climb into them, just in case they needed to leave the plane in a hurry.

When they were settled, they finished the Snickers bar in silence, checking for any sign of movement outside. After a while, May looked at her brother. Their faces were close, and when she spoke, he saw his breath around her head.

'They really know what you're thinking?'

Zak watched her. He was trying to decide if she was making fun of him.

'I mean it,' she said. 'I'm not winding you up. Seriously.'

Zak lowered his eyes. 'Yeah. I do think they know. And

it's really creepy, but it kind of makes sense. It explains so much.'

May waited for him to go on.

'The whole time we've been here I've been getting this feeling like something was inside my head. Or *trying* to get inside my head. Right from before we even landed. I've been seeing, like . . . ghosts. Of things I recognize. Things I've been thinking about.'

'Like what?'

'Like when we first arrived and we were talking about polar bears–'

'I remember.'

'So when we were going towards The Hub, I *saw* one. A polar bear.'

'There aren't any polar bears in–'

'I know that. But we'd been talking about them, and then I saw one.' Zak rubbed his face. 'I know how it sounds, but it looked real. I mean, it wasn't real, it was in my head, but it felt like it was there. I saw an explorer too, exactly like I'd seen in an old photo. Dad was talking about Scott of the Antarctic when we landed, so I was thinking about explorers and . . . it's like something rummaged through my head and found those thoughts. Like it was trying to break into my mind, so it used my *freshest* thoughts to make me understand it was there. Maybe it can't use words, so it uses pictures. And remember when the Spider attacked me in the Drone Bay?'

'How could I forget *that*?'

'It didn't hurt me, though, did it? But it was so weird, May,

I had, like, this vision of a sea of those bugs. The Spider was close' – Zak put his hand in front of his face – 'right here. So maybe the communication was stronger. Same as when I got close to the live bugs in the lab. And just now in Refuge. They felt stronger in my head, and . . . and I had this feeling like it wanted to tell me something, like there was something under the ice.'

'We know there's something under the ice, Zak.'

'But something *important*.' He paused. Maybe he'd said too much. The way she was looking at him, she probably thought he was going mad; that his illness was eating his brain and he'd finally lost the plot.

'You don't believe me,' he said. 'And don't give me that "I believe you believe it" rubbish–'

'I'm not!'

'– we both saw what those bugs did to Mum and Dad. And we've both seen those people out there acting like they're being controlled. The Spiders too, May. Those people found something under the ice and–'

'And now it wants to kill us,' May said.

Zak stopped and watched his sister. 'But it hasn't killed anyone yet, has it?'

'Not that we know of. So maybe it just wants to turn us into zombies.'

'But why?'

'Who cares why? To keep us for whatever's down there. Maybe it's some kind of alien.' May stared at Zak. 'And when it comes out, it's going to be hungry, so those bugs are making sure we don't go anywhere.'

Zak tried not to think about being eaten by aliens. 'Thing is, though, when we got here, the lights were out. If they wanted people to come here to get eaten, why would they make it difficult for us to land? And those emails . . . it's like something was trying to stop people from coming here. And when we needed heat, we got heat. When we needed light, we got light. So it doesn't make sense. Why would–'

'*None* of this makes sense, Zak.' There was frustration and fear in her voice. 'Bugs, zombies, robots coming to life. *None* of this makes sense. All I really want to know is how do we get out of here? How do we get Mum and Dad back?' May turned round and pointed her finger against the window. 'And how do we stop ourselves from either freezing to death or from getting turned into one of those things out there?'

Zak closed his eyes and took a deep breath. May was right. They were both getting cold. They wouldn't survive for long out here in the plane. But he tried not to think about the plane, because if he was right, something was watching his thoughts. The red-jackets would know by now that he and May weren't in Refuge, so they would be searching for them somewhere else. He pushed any picture of the plane from his mind and imagined them hiding in The Hub, on the upper level. He imagined them piling chairs and tables across the top of the stairs to barricade themselves in. It was difficult to keep the thought in his mind when there were so many other things to think about. He'd never realized how hard it was to think of two things at the same time.

Zak hung his head. It was such an impossible situation. Maybe it was time to give up. They'd be better off joining Mum and Dad and the others instead of being so scared all the time. It seemed so long ago that he was sitting in the plane, reading his book, hoping for an adventure.

Zak unzipped his left pocket and pulled out the paperback. He held it in both hands and stared at the cover. It was frayed now, from being stuffed in his jacket. The right corner was bent over, and there were a few scratches where he'd caught it on the zip. Jackson Jones would know what to do. He would have faced this whole nightmare with a witty remark and a few mishaps, but he wouldn't have given up. Jackson Jones never gave up.

Zak ran his fingers over the cover before shoving the book back into his pocket. 'OK, so we might not be able to figure out what they are or what they want, but I'm not going to let them take us without a fight. That's what Jackson Jones would do.'

'He's not real, Zak.'

'I know that, but we have to think like him. And the first thing he'd do is arm himself.' Zak raised the shovel. 'And I reckon the next thing he'd do is find a way to attack them. We've done nothing but run so far. Now it's time to find a way to fight.'

'How? There are too many,' May said. 'We can't fight *bugs*.'

'We have to go right to where they came from.'

'We don't know where they co– Wait, are you talking about the Storage place we saw on the video?'

Zak shook his head. 'Do you remember the map on the wall in The Hub?'

'Uh-huh.'

'On the right-hand side, it said "To The Chasm". I didn't think about it until just now but that's where they were taking the ice cores from. Sofia said that on the video. So if that's where the ice core came from, it must be where the bugs come from. There might be some kind of hive.'

'Oh, Zak, really? A hive?'

'I'm telling you, I'm right. *That's* where we have to go. *That's* where we destroy them. You have to listen to me. For once, you have to listen to me and do what I want.'

'Zak, it could be anywhere out there – if it even exists. And what are we going to do? Swipe them to death with our hammer and our snow shovel?

'All right, so maybe there's something else in here we can use. I don't know, May, I'm trying to be *brave* here. Trying to make a *plan*.'

'And I'm trying to be *realistic*.'

Zak was losing concentration. There were too many things to think about. 'I'm as scared as you are but we have to do something. We can't just sit here and freeze to death. We have to find a way to stop them; to get Mum and Dad back. We have to do *something*.'

May's face was drained of colour, and her lips were pale. Her teeth clicked gently as she shivered. 'You *are* brave, you know.'

'What?'

'You *are* brave. The bravest person I know.'

'But?' Zak was still trying to imagine him and his sister in The Hub, hiding from the bugs.

'But nothing,' she said. 'It's true. What you've got. The . . . you know. In your head.'

'The cancer.' Zak said it for her.

'Yeah. That. If *I* had that; if *I* was told about it like you were, I couldn't deal with it the way you did. You just got on with it, but I'd have been unbearable.'

'You already are.'

She snorted a short laugh.

'You're still my favourite sister, though.'

'You took it all in your stride.'

'It only looks that way,' Zak said.

'No, you accepted it and now look at you. You're being brave again. You're not scared; you want to fight these things. You're brave and you're tough.' May gave her brother a thin smile. 'Like Jackson Jones. I wish I was like that.'

Zak could hardly believe what he was hearing. 'You wish *you* were like *me*? No way. Those girls at school – Vanessa Morton-Chandler and the ones who hang around with her – they're mean to you all the time, but you just deal with them. I wish *I* was like *you*!'

May sighed. 'It's just an act. I pretend it doesn't bother me, them saying things and making stuff up, posting things online, but it does. It makes me feel . . .' She searched for the right words. 'Angry? Upset? I dunno. Embarrassed sometimes.'

'You don't let *them* see that, though. You don't give them the satisfaction.'

'I guess.'

'Same for me. I might not look scared but I *am* scared. I'm scared all the time. When I woke up in the French lesson that day, lying on the floor, seeing everyone staring at me, I was SO scared. The look on everyone's faces; they were . . . it freaked them out. It freaked *me* out. And then the doctor, and the drilling and . . . what if the treatment doesn't work? What if this thing keeps getting bigger? What if it fills my head? What if the doctors are wrong, and I die from it tomorrow?'

'Oh, Zak.' May's eyes glistened.

'But I hate being scared. I *hate* it. And the only way to stop being scared is to fight. So that's what we have to do now. We have to fight and–'

'What?' May turned to the window and saw what her brother had seen.

A group of red-jackets was advancing across the airstrip. Behind them, the Spider was making its way closer. *Tick-tack-tick-tack.*

'I'm sorry,' Zak said. 'I lost concentration. They've found us.'

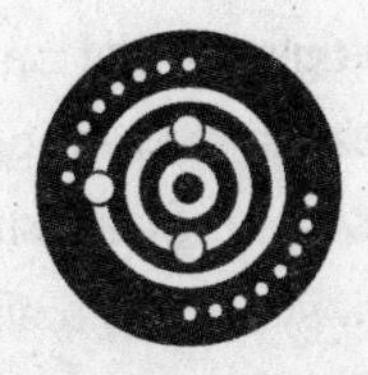

OUTPOST ZERO, ANTARCTICA
NOW

The monsters were coming.

A line of red-jackets was moving towards the plane, while the Spider waited by The Hub. There was nowhere left for Zak and May to run. There was nobody to help them. They might as well have been the only people left on earth.

May was swearing. A *lot.*

Zak gripped the shovel in both hands and moved along the plane. He was determined not to let anything happen to her: not just for her sake, but for his sake too – the last thing he wanted was to be left out there alone. He went to the ripped-open cockpit and squinted at the airstrip. The red-jackets were close, and Zak could hear the sound of their boots shuffling on the ice. It formed a kind of ugly beat along with the *tick-tack-tick-tack* of the Spider.

Zak leant the shovel against what was left of the instrument array and tugged one of the flares from his pocket. He popped off the cap and used it to scrape along the top of the red stick, as if he were lighting a giant match. The flare sparked first time and burst into life. It fizzed and hissed like a firework, bathing the cockpit in bright red light and white smoke. Zak threw it out on to the airstrip in front of the army of red-jackets who stopped as soon as it hit the ground. Zak lit two more and threw them out. They sputtered and popped, shedding a sinister red light across the ice. The smoke engulfed the red-jackets in an eerie, swirling cloud.

'The flares make them stop,' Zak shouted to his sister as he grabbed the shovel and planted his feet firm. He swung the weapon back over his shoulder, like a baseball bat, ready to smack the first person who tried to climb on board the trashed aircraft.

He watched the line of monsters standing in the red light and the churning smoke and, for the first time since seeing them, he realized they were not all wearing red jackets. Two of them were wearing orange jackets, just like his, and when he looked closely at their faces, his heart faltered.

Mum and Dad.

It was too horrible to think about. Attacked by his own mum and dad. The two people who were supposed to protect him. The people who should be keeping him safe. How could he defend himself against *them*? Would he be able to use the shovel against his own mum and dad?

It's not them, he told himself. *They're not Mum and Dad any more.*

Except, they *were* still Mum and Dad. And maybe this could be reversed. In his vision he had seen something big, a vast sea, and the more he thought about it, the more convinced he became that, whatever it was, it was under the ice. There was something down there that was doing this, controlling his mum and dad. And if he could find out what it was, if he could *stop* it, perhaps he could bring them back.

'Join us.'

Zak felt a darkening around the edges of his thoughts. A pain tightened behind his right eye. His vision wavered like he was dizzy, and he blinked hard, squeezing his eyes shut for a moment. 'No,' he whispered. 'Not now.'

The pain softened to an ache and Zak felt something probing at his thoughts. It was them. It. The hive. Whatever was under the ice was reaching out to him again, shuffling over his thoughts, trying to control him.

'Join us.'

'No.' He wouldn't join them. He refused. He tightened his grip on the shovel and concentrated on pushing the darkness away. 'Get out of my head.'

But it pushed harder into his mind, like a black sheet pulling across his thoughts. The ground fell away from beneath his feet as the familiar woozy floating sensation began to take over.

'Get out!' he shouted. 'Leave me alone!'

A blinding white light flashed in his mind and the darkness receded. Zak felt something trying to keep hold of his thoughts, but he was forcing it away, taking his mind back.

'We can't fight them,' May called from inside the plane. 'There's too many of them.'

On the airstrip, the flares were beginning to fizzle and die. Zak shook himself back into action. He held the shovel under his arm while he pulled another flare from his pocket, lit it, and threw it out on to the ice.

Only three left.

'Get up here quick,' Zak shouted to May as he struck another flare and threw it out. 'The flares are keeping them back. We still have time to jump down and run. If we can get to The Chasm, to the BioMesa place–'

'We don't know where it is!'

'What else can we do?'

The red-jackets stared at Zak. Their nightmarish slack faces, their skin tinted red in the light from the flares, their blank eyes reflecting the glow.

'Join us.' When they spoke, their words came out as one. Their breath puffed out around their heads and mingled with the smoke spiralling around them in the cold, cold air.

'Get back here,' May shouted. 'There's a door.'

Zak heard his sister moving about and he snatched a glance back into the plane. He could see her silhouette at the far end, struggling to push open the rear door.

Zak watched her for a second then turned back to the red-jackets. He pulled out one of his last two flares, preparing to light it.

'Mum.' His voice sounded small. As if Antarctica swallowed the words the moment they left his mouth. 'Dad. *Please*. Please stop doing this. It's me. Zak. You're scaring me. You have to fight it. Whatever's controlling you, making you like this, you have to fight it.'

Nothing. There was no change in their expression.

'The door!' May shouted. 'Come on!'

The flares stuttered and died and the ice was dark once more. The monsters took a step forwards. Advancing. This was the final attack.

'The door!'

Zak stuffed the unlit flare back into his pocket. He held the shovel tight as he ran along the length of the plane towards May. Skidding to a halt, he put his shoulder to the door and, together with his sister, they pushed as hard as they could. With a *click* and a *thump*, the door swung out and Zak and May tumbled on to the airstrip.

As soon as he hit the ground, Zak felt the pain probing in his head again. It was like a thick, blunt drill grinding into his skull, vibrating through his body. He tried to shake it away as he stumbled to his feet, reaching out to hold on to May. He grabbed her arm, hauling himself up, but when he opened his eyes, he saw he wasn't holding on to his sister.

Dima stared at Zak with a blank expression. 'Join us.'

They were waiting for us!

Zak pushed him away, sending the pilot stumbling into

the other red-jackets trying to surround him. He whirled around to see May struggling to free herself from the grip of two teenagers – a boy and a girl not much older than fifteen or sixteen. Already their jackets were writhing with movement and the bugs were beginning to emerge from their cuffs and hoods. They swarmed over their faces, pouring out from the warmth of their jackets and smothering Zak's sister.

'Help me!' May was shouting, but already the bugs were on her face, shedding their black armour, searching for a way in.

Zak shoved at a red-jacket who tried to attack him, and swatted at the bugs swirling in the air around them. He dropped low to grab the shovel. The blackness pushed into his thoughts again, the sound of the bugs amplifying by the second until his head was filled with the terrifying scuttle and buzz of a thousand legs and wings.

'Get out of my head!' he screamed as he swung the shovel hard.

The flat side struck something solid, sending a shock wave through Zak's body, but he didn't let it stop him. He swung again and again, turning in circles, insects thudding off the blade. 'Leave us alone!'

But there was no 'us'. Now there was only Zak.

May was gone. In his mad crazy dance of twirling and swiping, surrounded by insects, Zak saw May stop fighting. He saw the bugs push into her mouth and nose, and within seconds, she was one of those things like Mum and Dad.

He fought harder. He was the only one left now. With his mind, he tried to push out the darkness that wanted to take him away and hang him over the awful sea of writhing insects. And with the shovel, he swatted the bugs out of the air in front of him. And when he felt hands grabbing for him, clawing and pawing, he turned and hefted the weapon as hard as he could.

Zak hit one of the red-jackets square in the chest and the air went out of her. Her legs collapsed and she fell to the ice.

'Leave me alone!' he shouted as he swung at Dima, hitting him hard in the shoulder, the shovel sliding up and catching him against the side of the neck. The pilot's head snapped to one side and he collapsed like a felled tree. For an instant, Zak thought he had killed him, but as soon as he was on the ground, the pilot tried to get to his feet once more.

'Join us.'

Zak spun round and stared at his sister.

May's expression was blank. She was covered with bugs, but they were slipping inside her jacket, searching for the warmth.

'Join us,' she said again as hands reached for him, grasping at his arms.

The darkness was back, spreading over his thoughts. He was too close to them. He had to get away. He *had* to.

Zak turned and swung the shovel once more. He hit a teenage boy hard in the stomach, sending him reeling back. A girl came in to take his place, so Zak hit her and moved forwards, swinging the shovel left and right, whacking the flat of the blade against whoever or whatever got in his way. And as soon as he was free of them, he ran out on to the ice.

Escape. Escape.

He ran and ran and ran.

OUTPOST ZERO, ANTARCTICA
NOW

Zak Reeves was utterly alone.

He blundered away from the airstrip. His boots crunched icy snow, the *crump-crump-crump* the only sound in his head. Or rather, it was the only sound he *listened* to, because he blocked out the soft chanting of the red-jackets. No. Not just the red-jackets. May too. Mum and Dad. Dima. Their faces blank, their eyes empty, their bodies crawling with bugs.

He ran and ran, trying so hard to push their tortured faces from his mind. His legs moved as if they were on autopilot, because he needed all his mental strength to force the darkness from his head. It clouded in at the sides of his vision, made the world swim in front of him. The ground was hardly beneath him any more; it was softening, trying to fall away as the thing beneath the ice invaded his mind.

Zak had no idea he was shouting.

'Get out of my head!'

Over and over again.

'Get out of my head!'

Then it was gone. The probing fingers withdrew. His legs grew heavy – so, *so* heavy, like they were encased in concrete – but he continued to push across the snow, one foot at a time until he couldn't move another step and he fell to his knees and hung his head. His chest heaved, the cold air saturating his body, every breath blowing out his precious body heat. He let the tears flow, pooling in the base of his goggles, freezing solid on his cheekbones. He cried for Mum and Dad. He cried for May, and he cried for the hopelessness of his situation. There was no one to help him now. There was nowhere for him to go.

And when there were no more tears, Zak felt the cold tighten around him. He shivered hard and lifted his eyes to stare into the unforgiving desert.

Ahead of him, there was nothing.

Literally nothing. He heard May's voice as if she were right there with him.

The world stretched out for *ever*. On and on. Flat and cold and grey. If there had been enough light, it would have been brilliant white, but for now it was grey, grey, grey. To his right, another eternity of snow and ice. To his left, the same.

From somewhere out there, a rumbling reached out to him. The sound of an engine? Or was it something new? Something he hadn't seen? Perhaps it was another bio-mechanical monster, created by the Spiders. Or maybe it was help. Someone was coming? The sound grew louder as if it were approaching, but it passed to his left, too far out for him to see anything.

Zak sat up and listened, allowing himself a brief moment of faint hope, but as the sound faded to nothing, his hope of rescue faded with it. And when it was gone, he sat back in despair, wondering if the sound had even been real.

In the distance behind him, the base looked small. It looked *alien*, like he had run out on to a faraway planet. The lights were out again, so Outpost Zero was nothing but a series of shapes. Behind it, above the mountains, the sky was clear. A sickle moon sat low and bright, casting its silver light across the base. Ice and snow glittered like riches.

The moon was surrounded by a billion billion stars, burning through the atmosphere, bringing light that was millions of years old. But even that was nothing compared to the colour. The sky was *full* of colour. Pink, purple and yellow streaks shone upwards like searchlights, shifting and swirling among the stars. They swam across the heavens in moving shafts, filtering the glow of constellations, colouring the sky like a bioluminescent alien landscape.

The Aurora Australis.

Zak could hear Dad's voice in his head telling him what caused it. Something about electrons crashing into atoms in the atmosphere, but that made it sound so much less than it was. It made it boring. Actually *seeing* it was pure magic.

Zak shivered and tore his eyes away from the spectacle. He was wearing layers, good protection, but no kind of protection would last for ever out there. Already the cold was finding its way inside his clothes. He was losing body heat with every breath, and he could feel himself beginning to shiver more and more. He had to get inside. If he didn't find somewhere soon, he would freeze to death.

Zak got to his feet and turned in every direction. Nothing had changed. The landscape was still endless. It was still empty. He looked back at the base and wondered if there was any part of it that was safe, but he knew they were waiting for him. Wherever he went, whatever he did, they would sneak into his thoughts and they would *know*. The only place for him to go was towards The Chasm. Follow the arrow he had seen on the map. There had to be something there. If he could reach it, he might be able to find out what was happening here. He might be able to stop it.

So he checked his bearings with the silhouette of the base, and began walking out into the endless desert of Antarctica.

The cold was worsening. It stung his lungs and numbed his fingertips. He pulled his hood tighter, banged his hands together and rubbed them hard as he dragged his heavy feet on and on. His movement was slow and his steps were clumsy. And when he glanced back again, the base was tiny. If he lifted his hand he could pinch Outpost Zero between his finger and thumb as if it were a million miles away. There was no going back now, he would freeze to death before he reached it, but there was nothing ahead, either. Nothing but ice and snow and wind. And the realization crept over him with a deep feeling of dread. He had been wrong. The icy desert was as endless as space. He might as well have been searching for a single snowflake.

His mind was woozy, his thoughts confused. Everything was beginning to shut down. His senses were failing, but Zak knew enough to understand what was happening to him. Hypothermia was taking him in his grip. Killing him slowly. It was grinning as it wrapped its arms around him, squeezing tighter and tighter.

Come on in, Zak, it said. *Everyone's safe and warm in here*.

'Head back,' he mumbled, but Outpost Zero was nowhere to be seen now. He frowned and turned on the spot, watching the horizon, but there was nothing other than grey snow and black sky. The Aurora Australis was gone. Outpost Zero was gone. Zak had no idea which way to go.

Panic clutched at his heart. He *was* going to die out here. Like Scott of the Antarctic, he was going to freeze to death.

'Don't give up. You're almost there.'

Startled, Zak whipped around and stared at the figure standing not far away from him. It was the same person he had seen before, the one wearing ancient all-weather gear, like in those old photos. His head was covered by a woollen balaclava, with a hood pulled over it. Goggles protected his eyes.

'Who are you?' Zak was too tired to be afraid any more. 'What do you want?'

The figure didn't speak again. Instead, he lifted his right arm and beckoned with his hand.

'You want me to follow?'

The figure turned and walked away.

So Zak followed. His feet dragged, and his body shivered. He had no idea where he was going, and he wasn't sure if he even cared. He just didn't want to be alone and he didn't want to die. But his body was starting to fail him. He couldn't feel his face, his fingers were numb, and his legs were growing weaker by the second. His mind was vague and unfocused. The cold was forcing its way in. Hypothermia was winning, and Zak began to think dying wouldn't be so bad. If he gave up and fell into the snow to lie still and let the cold take him, all of this would be over. All the fear and the pain would disappear.

What a relief that would be.

But he didn't stop. He trudged on and on, following the figure towards a rise in the perfect landscape. And as he came closer, Zak turned his head slowly left and right, peering along the length of the ridge. It was at least a hundred metres high, and stretched as far as he could see in both directions. A perfect white wall with smooth sides. The only way to climb it would be with ropes and spikes.

He had reached a dead end.

'Why?' Zak shivered violently and looked at the figure that had led him here, but instead of seeing the ancient explorer, with its face covered like a ghoul, he saw his sister.

May.

Now I know I'm going mad . . .

She wasn't dressed as she had been when he last saw her. Instead, she was dressed how he best remembered her. Tight black jeans with knees so ripped it was a wonder they didn't fall apart when she wriggled into them. A black T-shirt with *The Walking Dead* printed in bold white letters. A leather biker jacket with pin badges on the lapels. One of the pins was completely yellow, such a happy colour, with two black dots for eyes and a big smiley mouth. There was a splash of red blood on one side. She wore her favourite Dr. Martens boots, and a black beanie with a picture of a white hand holding a red heart-shaped hand grenade. Her hair was hanging loose from the edges of the beanie.

May had her arms crossed and was staring at her brother as if she couldn't understand why the cold was bothering him so much. 'Come on, you loser, what are you waiting for?'

Zak didn't know if she was actually there, or if he was even hearing her voice for real. He had seen so many bizarre things over the past few hours, this was just another one to add to the long list.

'What are you waiting for?' May spoke (*thought?*) again, and a wide door slid open in the endless white wall beside her. When the door was open enough for a person to pass through, May lifted a hand and swept it towards the entrance and the darkness it had revealed. 'Get inside, you freak. You're the only one who can see this. The only one we can tell. You're the only one who can know.'

Zak frowned and hesitated. It might be some kind of trap, but what did he have to lose? There was nowhere else for him to go.

So he stumbled forward, and followed May into the unknown.

Zak found himself in a rectangular room carved into the ice. White light shone from tiny bulbs fitted into the perfectly square corners, and an Arctic Cat snowmobile sat idle by the door. On the other side of the room a sloped corridor led deeper into the ice. There was no heat to warm his body, and Zak struggled to control his shivering as he followed his sister along the ice-corridor. A harsh draught moaned around him like the ghosts of the unhappy dead.

Zak made his way down and down, deeper and deeper into the ice until he came to a vast cavern with perfectly smooth walls of ice and a high, flat ceiling. The space was at least three times as big as the assembly hall at school, but instead of being stuffed with stacked chairs and smelling like school dinners, it was filled with horrors and stank like a slaughterhouse.

Bugs, like the ones that had smothered Mum, Dad and May, were everywhere. They crawled along the walls, they carpeted the floor, they clicked and rustled and fluttered as they scuttled over each other or took to the air. Littered among the insects covering the floor, there were parts taken from the dismantled plane and Magpie, and cobbled-together machines clattered with gears and glistened with grey cords of muscle, but all these were dwarfed by the giant monster towering over them.

Zak guessed it had been one of Mum and Dad's Spiders, but it was hardly recognizable now. Instead of shining steel and alloy, the drone was encased in a hard outer shell similar to the kind covering the bugs. Grey translucent sinews twisted at its joints, and criss-crossed the creature's underside. The monster was a demented mix of mechanical and biological. Metal pincers protruded from its face, coarse hairs growing around them. It was part-Spider, part-bug, all gross. Insects swarmed over it, disappearing beneath the shell, crawling over its fleshy parts, shedding their armour and melting into the monster, becoming part of it. They were giving it life. The smell rising from it was like wet soil and fresh meat.

On the other side of the cavern, opposite the corridor, May stood in a place where the world fell away into nothing. An immense and jagged rip ran from left to right like a monstrous mouth, its edges like dangerous teeth. A tear in the ice so wide it was impossible to see the other side.

The Chasm.

Zak crossed the huge room and went to his sister. He peered over the edge of The Chasm and stared into the endless depths of the Earth, thinking that if he toppled forwards and fell, he would be falling for ever. But the longer he stared into its eternity, the more he began to see.

There was something moving down there. Flickering fluorescent lights flitting backwards and forwards like fireflies in the darkness.

'Let us show you.' May spoke again, but Zak knew it wasn't May, and when he looked at her, she faded and shimmered like an old memory. She was an illusion, put into his head by something he didn't understand, but she was trying to tell him something. Whatever lay beneath the ice, it *wanted* Zak to understand.

Zak stared down into The Chasm once more, and saw the flickering lights lifting towards him like tiny lanterns in the night. The hum of insects grew louder as the swarm approached from below, and then they were rising up, surrounding him. And as they covered his body, Zak felt warm, and the familiar darkness of another vision came to him. But he no longer felt afraid, and this time he didn't fight it. Instead, he let his mind go.

Zak surrendered himself to the vision.

OUTPOST ZERO, ANTARCTICA
NOW

As the vision slipped over him, Zak was surrounded by darkness so complete, so *solid*, that it was as if he was buried deep in fine black powder. Except, it felt like he was floating. Like his mind wasn't in his body any more.

Weirdest. Feeling. *Ever.*

Zak wondered if he was dying.

No. This isn't death. This is something else. This isn't even real. This is all in my head. This is the vision – the thing they've been trying to show me.

Standing on the edge of The Chasm, with insects crawling over him, Zak's mind joined with theirs, and he saw everything they wanted him to see. Their message came to him in a flash of images, racing through his thoughts.

He saw lights moving in the darkness below him, thousands of insects flickering and fluttering in the freezing, black depths. He saw a river of them flowing through the ice beneath his feet, swarming over each other, their legs intertwining, their wings struggling to open in the tight space. And the mind of every single insect was connected to the mind of every other insect, all of them acting together as if they were one.

I was right. A hive *mind.*

And now, in a way, he was part of that collective mind too. They could reach his thoughts in a way they couldn't reach anybody else at Outpost Zero.

Because I'm different. My mind *is different.*

His illness weakened him; it made him vulnerable.

The insects showed him the river of seething bugs flowing away beneath the ice, flooding into a shimmering, glowing *sea* of them. A sea that pulsed with a fluorescent glow. The number of insects was impossible to grasp. More than thousands. More than millions. More than *billions.* All of their minds connected. All of them trying to free themselves from the ice directly below Outpost Zero.

BioMesa had discovered them, and now they had to protect themselves. They had to survive. They had to escape and find somewhere new – somewhere safe to hibernate.

And in the vision, Zak saw how their light was creating great heat, melting the ice that entombed them. The insects were almost ready to escape, but above them, Outpost

Zero was perched on ice that was growing thinner and thinner.

Their freedom would destroy Outpost Zero. That was what they wanted to tell him. They wanted to warn him.

But what are you? Zak needed to understand.

So the insects showed him.

A blinding blast of light and heat erupted in his mind, and in that energy, a billion tiny explosions created a cloud of gas that twisted and snaked like the tendrils of a smoky giant. When the gas faded into nothing, Zak saw the cold darkness of space, he saw planets form and break apart, he saw stars burning bright in the unreachable distance.

This is the beginning of everything, he thought. *This is how the universe began. Why are you showing me this?*

More images flashed through his mind like a movie played on fast-forward behind his eyelids. He felt as if he were cascading among the planets, passing through rock and space and stars, gaining speed, faster, faster, until it was impossible to focus, and everything was a blur of dark, light, time, energy and–

Everything stopped.

For a second, his thoughts were blank, and then his mind was filled with an image of a planet hanging in space. Earth.

On the surface of the planet, a swirling, white-crested blue sea crashed and foamed. Above it, two spirals of light twisted around each other, a double helix of glowing insects rising up. And as the insects reached the top of the spirals, they shed their hard casings, letting their bodies fall to the ocean, decomposing into a soup of cells that split and grew and became life.

Every creature on the planet came from these insects. The information Dad found in the lab – the DNA, the genomes, the stem cells – that's what the insects were. They were the beginning of all life on earth, and in his vision Zak saw their cells grow into mammals, reptiles, birds, fish, insects . . . *everything*.

When Zak opened his eyes, he was back in the ice-cavern. The insects had returned to The Chasm, but Zak felt the ghost of their presence in his mind. He felt remnants of their fleshy bodies on his face, their life-creating cells soaking into his skin. It ran warm in his veins, moving through his body, filling his mind. He felt a calming release of pressure inside his brain, and when he looked around, he saw the world with new eyes. The insects had more right to be here than he did.

'I think I understand,' Zak said. 'I think I know what you are.'

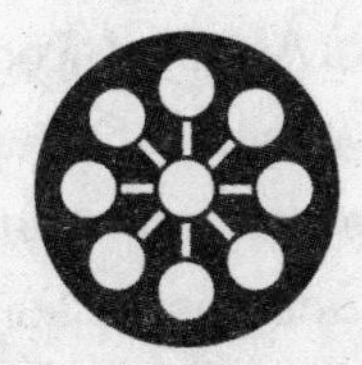

APPROACHING OUTPOST ZERO, ANTARCTICA
NOW

'We're about thirty minutes out,' the pilot said.

Lazarovich leant forward to see along the interior of the Osprey and into the cockpit.

'Storm's passed, weather's looking good,' Captain Jackson continued. 'Maybe we'll reach Zero a little ahead of time. Approaching from the south.'

'Copy that.' Lazarovich settled back into her seat and cast her eyes over the other operatives sitting either side of the Osprey interior.

Every one of them was faceless behind the visor of his or her battle helmet, but her own visor sensed who she was looking at, and their name appeared, as if by magic, floating in her vision. She didn't need it though, didn't need the technology to tell her who they were – Lazarovich knew them as well as she knew herself. She knew their strengths, their weaknesses, their build, their mannerisms. She had worked with them, lived with them, trained them. If they had all been wearing overalls, standing in a darkened room with sacks on their heads, Lazarovich could have picked out each one of them by name.

What she didn't know was what to expect when she landed at Outpost Zero. As usual, Phoenix had given her as little information as possible. Secure the base, secure whatever those people had found under the ice, eliminate everyone, and await further instruction.

Most of it sounded straightforward – if there was one thing Lazarovich and her team knew how to do, it was to secure an enemy placement and leave no survivors – but one part of it was bothering her. The 'secure whatever those people had found under the ice' part. Something about it felt . . . off.

An alert symbol appeared in the top right of her visor display. The word '**PHOENIX**' was written beside it.

'Open message,' Lazarovich said, and an image popped up in place of the alert. It appeared to be hovering in the air on the other side of the cabin.

Lazarovich studied the updated thermal satellite image. It was immediately obvious that the heat signature below the ice had grown. The river of red now stretched from The Chasm in the east, all the way across to the centre of the natural basin in the land, where it ballooned. Outpost Zero was right in the centre of it, as if it were hanging over a giant sea of lava. Whatever was down there was big. *Huge.* Securing something that size could be problematic, especially when they didn't even know what it was.

The airstrip was showing as pale blue on the edge of the red sea. It was cold and hard, ready for a good landing, but the Storage building was glowing dull orange – they would need to check it out. Lazarovich was thinking it might be where the base personnel were hanging out.

'Close image.' The image disappeared. 'Open comms.' Lazarovich waited for the click to indicate she was speaking to the whole team. 'OK, listen up everyone. We're thirty minutes out. Time to wake up, stop thinking about your comfy beds back home and your families waiting for you. I need full concentration.' She paused. 'I want a clean dispersal when we touch down. We'll secure the landing zone. Team Two, you take The Hub, split two ways and sweep in both directions. You know the layout, I want the East and West Tunnels cleared. Eliminate everything. Team One with me on the ice – we'll maintain the landing zone and sweep the outlying Storage building, then we'll see what we've come all this way for. I want this clean, clear and careful. No casualties on our side. All eyes open and alert; I've got a bad feeling about this.'

'Leader, you always say that.'

'I know.' Lazarovich focused on the operative sitting opposite her. 'But this time I mean it.'

JANUARY ISLAND, SOUTH CHINA SEA
NOW

The lights were dimmed in The Broker's 'War Room' and the temperature was exactly how he liked it. Beside him, on the table, was a mug of green tea. The design on the mug said 'World's Best Dad'. He picked it up without taking his eyes off the ultra-high-definition screens on the wall in front of him.

The display on the left showed a regularly updated satellite image of Outpost Zero. On the right, the last ten images were stacked together so he could see the growth of what was beneath the ice. Whatever it was, it had begun to increase in size at an incredible rate.

The centre screens showed images fed directly from Lazarovich's team. Each operative had a camera set into their battle helmet so The Broker could watch them every step of the way. He never spoke to them, never communicated with them, but he was always watching. He saw what they saw.

Their eyes were his eyes.

The Broker sat back and cleared his throat. He raised his mug, but before it touched his lips he stopped and glanced at his hand. There was a slight tremble there, the tea rocking from side to side. He smiled, and allowed himself a moment to enjoy the buzz of nervous anticipation. After all, life and death was about to unfold on the screens in front of him. What could be more exciting than that?

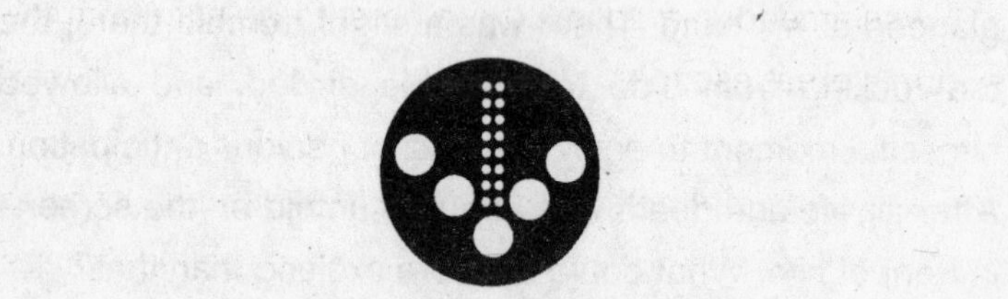

OUTPOST ZERO, ANTARCTICA
NOW

Zak left The Chasm with a sense of wonder. He wasn't forced to leave. His body wasn't controlled, and his mind was his own. He left because he knew he was safe from the hive below the ice, and that Mum and Dad and May would be safe too. He knew the people of Outpost Zero would be safe as long as they stayed in Storage. And he knew what the insects wanted.

He crossed the ice-cavern, and made his way up the incline towards the large door he had first entered through. As he reached the top, the door slipped open and Zak looked out across the calm desert of snow and ice stretched in front of him. In the distance, Outpost Zero was crowned by the green and purple glow of the Aurora. He watched the lights dancing in the sky, then glanced at the Arctic Cat snowmobile beside him.

He had driven something similar once before, so he climbed on and turned the key. The engine jumped into life. Zak twisted the throttle and drove the snowmobile out on to the ice. He accelerated away from The Chasm, closing the distance to Outpost Zero in just a few minutes.

It was time for him to join the others; to be safe from the swarm's great escape.

The air inside Storage was warm and there was enough light for Zak to make out the silhouettes of the figures standing at the far end of the room. Dima was there, some of the others he had seen out on the ice too. Mum and Dad and May were standing at the front, eyes closed as if they were in a peaceful sleep.

'It'll all be over soon,' Zak said as he approached them. 'I don't think it's going to be long now.'

They remained motionless, eyes closed.

'You should have seen it,' Zak said to May, leaning in to whisper in her ear. 'It was amazing. Kind of gross, but amazing.'

Something moved behind him and he turned to scan the room.

There were boxes here and there, crates and other paraphernalia. Some of them were open, the contents piled up as if someone had been digging through them. And there was something else – something in the shadows at the side of the room, half-hidden by a stack of boxes. Zak frowned and leant forward, trying to see. At first he thought it might be the explorer, and he wondered why the insects needed to show him that again.

'Stay right there,' it said. 'Don't move an inch.'

Zak recognized the voice. It carried a familiar Australian twang.

Could it really be her?

'Sofia?' Zak peered into the shadow. 'Is that you? You're alive?'

There was a pause. 'You know me?'

'Oh my God, I can't believe you're alive!' Zak said. 'That's so cool! We found your video. You uploaded it to ViBac and–'

'Why aren't you like them?'

'I . . .' *Because I'm different. My brain is different.*

'Get over here,' Sofia said without waiting for an answer. 'Don't wake them up.'

'No, honestly, it's fine. They're–'

Sofia came forward like a moray eel darting out from its lair beneath a rock. She grabbed Zak by the front of his jacket, and retreated, pulling him into the darkness.

'Don't you dare wake them up,' she said. 'Don't you *dare*. When Peters and I set them off, I thought they'd never stop but I've managed to get in and out of here a few times without starting them off again, so don't you go getting them all riled up.'

Zak thought it best to agree. This close up, he could see

Sofia's eyes and she looked crazy. Scared and mad.

'How did you avoid them?' she asked. 'I saw you lot land. Watched you get off the plane and go into the base. I tried to make contact, but I couldn't get past the Spiders. A few hours later four of you are in here – but not you.'

'They're going to be OK. Everything is going to be OK.'

'Wait a minute.' Sofia grabbed Zak again and spun him round, staring at the back of his neck. 'Have you got one of those things on you?'

'No.' Zak struggled against her.

'Something in your nose, then.' Sofia spun him round again and leant close to peer up his nostrils. 'What are you people even doing here?'

Zak pushed her away. 'Will you listen to me?'

'No, you listen to me. I watched you go out on to the ice. I saw you go into that BioMesa place at least . . .' She checked her watch. 'An hour ago and–'

'Wait. You *saw* me?' Zak remembered how he had heard an engine out on the ice. 'You were on a snowmobile, weren't you? And you left me out there. You didn't help me.'

'Don't change the subject. Anyway, of course I tried to help you. I saw the others get caught and you ran off on to the ice. When the Spider was gone, I came after you, tried to find you, but when I did, you were already on your way inside the BioMesa place. There's no way I was going in there again. Not after what I saw last time. I thought you were a goner for sure.'

'You've seen?' Zak asked. 'You've been down there?'

Sofia took hold of Zak's arm and pulled him towards the

window. On the other side of the landing strip, one of the Spiders was making its way across the ice, heading out towards The Chasm.

'The other two are still in there. *Down* there.' Sofia said. 'And there goes the third one. I've been watching them going in and out since the start of this, coming back for I don't know what. To recharge, find new parts, something like that. But a while back, all those Spiders were up here, tearing your plane to pieces, so I went over there and saw those bugs and . . . they were everywhere. Now, I don't know what they are, but they are *not* good . . . and I reckon there's a whole ton more of them under the ice. Maybe something else too. Something big and bad that wants to get out, and those Spiders are helping to set it free.'

'It's not bad,' Zak said. 'They're just trying to–'

'So I rigged the whole thing with HEX 13,' Sofia stopped him. 'They're only small pieces but it's enough to blow that whole place to bits. Bring the roof in and kill everything inside it. I've been waiting for them all to go back down. Get them all at once and put an end to this. Only thing that stopped me was seeing you go in there, but you're here now, and you seem OK so . . .' Sofia raised her left hand to show Zak something similar to a smartphone. In large white letters it displayed the word 'CONFIRM' and beneath it, a glowing dot traced across the screen in the shape of a letter Z. Sofia put her finger to the screen. 'All I've got to do is swipe here and . . . Boom.'

'No.' Zak grabbed her hand. 'You can't.'

'Can't? What do you mean "can't"? I'm guessing that's your mama and papa, right?' She pointed at the people standing at the back of the room.

'Yes, but–'

'Then it's time to put an end to it.'

'They're not what you think,' Zak said quickly. 'The insects. They're not what you think. They're like . . . an Ark.'

'What?'

'An Ark.' Now he'd said it, the word felt so right. It was the perfect way to describe what was under the ice. 'Like in the story, except instead of being a boat full of animals, it's a swarm. A whole hive of insects full of DNA and genomes and . . .' Zak was trying to remember all the things he had seen on the tablet computer in the lab. 'And stem cells and . . . I don't know. *Stuff*. All the stuff needed to make life on Earth.'

'You saying they're some kind of alien?'

'No. They belong here. They've always been here. They're us. They're everything. They're where *life* came from.'

Sofia backed away from Zak, holding the detonator high out of his reach. She glanced out of the window, seeing the Spider disappear from view. A few more minutes and it would enter the cavern. Sofia would have them all in her trap. 'What are you talking about?'

'I saw it,' Zak said. 'They showed me. When they shed their armour, they kind of melt into a grey mush that's full of cells and DNA and stuff to make life. They're trying to protect themselves. They don't want to hurt anybody, so they moved everyone over here, where it's safe for us. They just want to survive. They want *us* to survive.'

Sofia watched Zak as if he'd gone mad.

'All they want is a bit more time and then they'll go somewhere else. Somewhere they'll be safe. They were never supposed to be found. They're not ready.'

'Ready for what?'

'To make life again.'

'What the hell are you talking about?'

'Ugh!' Zak grunted with frustration. How could he make her understand when she didn't want to listen? He wished he could show her what he had seen. How was he supposed to describe the beginning of the world? How could he explain that the hive contained everything necessary for new life? That they were the most ancient and vital part of the planet? That without them, Earth would be dry and dead? And that when humans wasted the planet and were dead and gone, these insects would breathe new life into it?

Zak closed his eyes and concentrated. He focused on the images he had seen, and tried to project them, to make Sofia see them too. He felt a release of tension in his mind, as if something that had been weighing him down had been lifted away.

'I'm sorry, kid.' Sofia put her thumb on the detonator switch. 'I have to do this. It's the only–'

'Stop.' Zak opened his eyes and touched her hand.

Sofia paused with her thumb millimetres above the screen.

'Don't do it.'

Unable to tear her eyes from Zak's gaze, Sofia lifted her thumb away from the screen.

'Give it to me.' Zak held out his other hand and Sofia lowered the device towards it.

Outside, the sound of distant thunder rumbled; a noise that distracted Zak, making him turn to the window. Sofia blinked hard, as if she had woken from a dream to find herself somewhere unexpected. 'What the–?'

The sound grew louder, distracting Sofia the same way it had distracted Zak. She stopped mid-sentence, her confusion deepening, then her eyes lit up and she moved quickly, putting her face to the window. 'Rescue.' She grinned. 'Someone's coming. And they're coming *fast*!'

The noise increased like an approaching freight train until it filled Zak's head with a pounding rhythmic pulse. Storage began to vibrate, the walls shaking, the shelves wobbling. Canisters toppled and clattered to the floor. Tools danced in their toolboxes, rattling and jumping together.

'Sounds like a hundred helicopters,' Sofia shouted. 'They've sent the cavalry!'

The noise became a deafening roar, right above their heads, and when Zak put his face to the glass and looked up, the nose of a large aircraft nudged into view. As it passed over, he saw the large wing and the two engines like the rotors of a helicopter.

'That's an Osprey,' Sofia thought aloud. 'Or something like it. Biggest one I've ever seen. I'm pretty sure Exodus doesn't have anything like that. Maybe it's BioMesa.'

The aircraft hovered over them, half in view, and another thundered past it, flying over the airstrip and hanging in the air.

'We're going to be OK,' Sofia said. 'Help's arrived.'

OUTPOST ZERO, ANTARCTICA
NOW

The two aircraft rumbled as they hovered over Outpost Zero. They drifted in circles, sweeping the ground with powerful searchlights before separating and moving to opposite ends of the landing strip, where they began to descend. A storm of snow kicked up as they neared the ground, and Zak couldn't tell if they had landed or not until the rhythmic thump of their engines cut out and the base fell silent.

Inside Storage, Sofia put a hand on Zak's shoulder and stood to look out of the window. 'Well done. You guys must have got a message out,' she said without taking her eyes off what was happening outside.

'No.' Zak brushed her hand away and manoeuvred himself so he could see better. 'No we didn't. Nothing worked.'

'You sure?'

'Positive.'

'Well, that's weird, then. 'Cause I didn't get a message out either.' She bit her bottom lip as the flurries of snow settled and the aircraft became visible through the glass.

One was positioned at either end of the landing strip, facing away from the base. In perfect coordination, the back door on both aircraft lowered and six figures emerged from each one.

'So now I'm wondering who *they* are. Because they definitely don't look like science nerds from Exodus.'

Zak couldn't agree more. The figures were dressed in heavy white combat trousers and jackets, marked with light grey camouflage patterns. They wore helmets with blue-tinted visors covering their faces, and each had a pack on his back and an assault rifle in his hands. To Zak, they were more like Imperial Stormtroopers landing on Hoth, than scientists.

'Soldiers.' Sofia ducked so she was peering out of the bottom of the window. 'And that kit looks state of the art.'

Zak ducked too, and watched the tactical teams fan out from the aircraft, finding good arcs of fire to cover all angles of the base. Some dropped to one knee while others remained upright, rifles pointed ahead of them. They paused, scanning the area as a thirteenth figure emerged from the darkness of the aircraft to Zak's right, and strode out on to the ice.

The thirteenth soldier was not dressed the same way as the others – this one wore black from head to toe, with a red-tinted visor on a shining black battle helmet. Faceless. Anonymous. Terrifying.

From the way the figure moved, Zak was pretty sure she was a woman. Tall and strong in her combat gear, she had a large weapon slung over her back and carried an assault rifle. She moved out to stand between the two teams, and turned in a circle, inspecting the base, before raising a hand. Immediately, the team that had emerged from the aircraft to Zak's left, reformed and headed towards The Hub. Within less than a minute, they had entered Outpost Zero and were gone.

The second team remained outside.

'They know what they're doing.' Sofia glanced at the detonator still in her hand. 'Maybe I won't need this after all.'

'You can't use that,' Zak said. 'You have to believe me. The hive doesn't want to hurt us. But them . . .?' He tapped the window. 'I'm not so sure about them. I've got a horrible feeling. I don't think they're the cavalry.'

'Then who are they?' Sofia studied Zak's expression.

'I don't know, but they look dangerous.'

Sofia turned to watch the operatives again. 'Oh yeah, they definitely look dangerous.'

'The Exodus Project is all about living on Mars,' Zak said. 'Not fighting. Why would they have people like that?'

The air seemed to go out of Sofia. 'I *so* want that to be

the cavalry, but right now my gut is agreeing with your gut. There's something not right about this. But if they're not Exodus, then who are they? BioMesa? And what do they want?'

Outside, the second team of operatives was splitting into two groups, one team of three heading towards Storage, weapons raised.

'They're coming here!' Zak couldn't take his eyes off their guns. 'What do we do?'

Sofia looked at the kid beside her, seeing how scared he was. She was scared too, but she also felt something else – guilt. This was her fault. If she hadn't taken Jennings' card and gone out to The Chasm that day – if she had left core #31 alone – this would never have happened. She'd probably be in The Hub right now playing video games with Pablo, or one of the others. And this kid here . . .

'What's your name?' she asked.

'Zak.'

. . . and *Zak* would be safe with his mum and dad instead of being terrified and stuck in here with her.

She had to do something.

'I'll go out there,' Sofia said. 'Let them know we're here.'

'What? No!'

'We don't have any choice. They're going to be in here in a few minutes anyway. What else can we do?'

'Hide?'

'*Where?* There isn't anywhere to hide, and we don't want to surprise them. I reckon it's better to go out and talk to them.'

'I . . .'

'If we surprise them, they'll probably shoot us. Look, I'll go out there,' Sofia said. 'You stay here.' She held out the detonator. 'Keep hold of this.'

Zak stared at the device and shook his head. A few minutes ago he had been trying to make Sofia give it to him, but he didn't want it any more; didn't want the responsibility of what it could do. What if he detonated it by accident? What if–

'Take it.' Sofia grabbed his hand and pressed the detonator into it.

'You can't go out there,' Zak said.

'They're going to find us whether I go out there or not. So you stay here and I'll go out. Hopefully they're friendly, but if they're not, I'll give you a signal–'

'What signal?'

'I don't know, I'll think of something, and when I do you need to trace your finger along this symbol.' Sofia pointed at the device in his hand. On the screen, the white dot was still zigzagging in a Z pattern. 'That's all there is to it.'

'But the hive,' Zak said. 'It'll blow up the–'

'Yeah. And it might distract those fellas out there long enough to buy us time to . . . Well, I dunno, but it's all we've got.'

'I can't.' Zak stared at the detonator. 'I can't do that.'

'Let's hope you don't have to.' Sofia patted him on the shoulder and went to the door. 'Wish me luck.' She pressed the button and stepped out.

*

The soldiers spotted Sofia as soon as she left Storage, but it was the woman in black who shot her.

She raised her rifle to her shoulder, aimed and fired. The movement took her no more than a second.

Sofia dropped to her knees at the bottom of the steps. She stayed upright, swaying, then fell forward into the snow and lay still.

No!

The soldiers moved forwards, the woman in black marching across the ice like a shadow. Like Death. She was gesturing with her left hand, giving orders, pointing at Storage. The other soldiers fanned out as they approached.

Watching from the window, Zak was reeling from what he had seen. These people, these *monsters*, were far worse than anything else he'd had to endure here at Outpost Zero. They had killed Sofia as if she were nothing, without saying a word, and now they were coming to get him.

They would kill him like they had killed Sofia, and they would do the same to everyone else.

Mum. Dad. May.

Everyone.

He stared at the detonator in his hand. Sofia had said he should use it to buy himself some time, but with his finger over the 'Z', ready to set it off, he thought of what it would do . . . of all the life it would destroy. Life that only wanted to survive. And he came to a decision. No matter the situation, he couldn't harm what was beneath the ice. He put the detonator on the ground and smashed his heel into it. He would not destroy the Ark. And if he protected It, perhaps It would protect him.

Please, Zak thought. *Please don't let this be happening.* He had pleaded like this before, without realizing it, but he meant it now more than he had ever meant it. He had begged for help when they were in the plane, when he had wished for the lights to come on so they could land safely. He had begged for it again, when they needed light and power in the base. He had made wishes and his wishes had been granted. In The Hub, after Dima fell down the stairs, May had said it was weird, but it hadn't been magic, it had been *them*. He was sure of it now. His mind was connected to those things breaking out from under the ice, and they had helped him when he most needed it. And if they had helped him before, they would help him now.

Please, he thought again. *Help us. Help us and we'll help you.*

You have to help. Please.

The woman in black led her soldiers closer and closer, weapons ready and trained at the door and the window, but Zak tried to not to think about her. He tried not to think about Sofia lying dead on the ice. He tried to crush his fear inside him. He concentrated on projecting his thoughts, hoping the insects would see them. That they would come. He imagined the same image over and over again.

A swarm. He needed a swarm.

But he didn't get a swarm. Instead, the three Spiders appeared from the far end of the airstrip, horrifying and beautiful all at once. Huge and imposing, they moved quickly across the ice, like living, breathing beasts of metal and muscle. They covered the ground at amazing speed, bearing down on the soldiers.

As they raced across the ice, the woman in black heard them or sensed them, Zak couldn't know, but she turned, whipping her rifle round and firing without hesitation. The weapon kicked in her hands and Zak saw the muzzle flash. The other soldiers did the same, and as they opened fire, the operatives who had entered The Hub emerged back on to the ice, drawn by the sound of battle.

Bullets thumped into the attacking Spiders. They cracked the composite, ricocheted from the steel, dented the aluminium and sank into the flesh. Each hit caused more damage than the last.

Zak had no idea who the soldiers were, but what they had done to Sofia told him all he needed to know. They were not here to help, they were here to kill. And the machines he had once been so afraid of were now his only hope. He no longer saw them as monsters, but as his saviours.

The Spiders reached the Osprey at the east side of the airstrip and began to close the distance between them and the soldiers. They only had to withstand a few more seconds of fire.

They're going to save us.

The soldiers concentrated their attack, trying to force the Spiders back with a wall of bullets. The machines jerked and juddered under the impact, their progress slowing, but they were getting closer. They were gaining ground.

The Ark is going to save us.

Just a few more *seconds* and . . . the woman in black dropped her rifle and unslung the large weapon from her back. Bulky and deadly, Zak knew what it was. He'd played enough video games to recognize a grenade launcher when he saw one.

The woman in black tucked the stock against her shoulder and fired.

There was a short pause – less than a second – and the explosive detonated in front of the oncoming Spiders in a blast of ice and fire. The eruption shredded the muscular machines, blowing them into a thousand pieces. Their legs ripped away, their bodies shattered, and pieces of them tore across the ice in all directions. Burning fragments pounded the closest Osprey, like hellfire, and a second explosion erupted with a muted *WHUMP!* as the Osprey's fuel tanks ignited in a huge ball of orange flames. The blast tore the aircraft in half, spinning it around on the landing strip as the fuel tanks beneath the second wing detonated. The air was filled with fire and smoke and heat as shrapnel blasted out in all directions. It thumped against the Storage building like heavy rain and Zak ducked as the reinforced glass shattered and sprayed fragments into the room.

The machines that had taken so long to build, that had been given life by something ancient and pure, were torn to pieces in a few seconds. They were nothing but broken parts.

And for Zak, all hope was lost.

OUTPOST ZERO, ANTARCTICA
NOW

One end of the airstrip was ablaze. The Osprey was twisted like a broken toy, black smoke pouring from the wreckage, and there were huge potholes where the aircraft had exploded. But the soldiers didn't waste a moment.

Within a few seconds of the Spiders' destruction, the woman in black was signalling to her people, issuing new commands. After a pause, one team split away and headed back into The Hub. The other soldiers fanned out across the airstrip as if they were protecting the remaining aircraft.

Zak couldn't breathe.

Sofia was dead. There was no way out of Storage, and there was nothing he could use to defend himself. Not that he'd ever be able to defend himself against *her*.

Outside, the woman in black raised the weapon to her shoulder and aimed it at Storage. Zak saw it clearly from where he was standing, and he knew exactly what it would do.

In a few seconds he would be nothing.

But as the woman in black prepared to incinerate the building, the ground began to tremble. At first it was a gentle sensation accompanied by a low rumble that made the woman pause and look back, but it was growing stronger. Louder.

Storage shook, the contents of the shelves rattling as they had done when the aircraft were directly overhead. The ground moved beneath Zak's boots and, outside, the woman in black side-stepped and put out her arms like a tightrope walker trying to keep balance.

Zak stumbled too, grabbing at the wall, trying to stay on his feet. Containers clattered. Supplies shifted and fell over. Cans rolled off the shelves. Mum and Dad and May bumped into the red-jackets as they swayed together, knees buckling, falling in a heap.

An earthquake. The thought flashed through Zak's head. *Saved by an earthquake.*

Outside, a sharp crack split the air and Zak clung to the edge of the window, peering out at the soldiers who had dropped low to avoid falling over. The woman in black had her back to Storage now and was signalling orders. The rumbling was growing louder by the second, and The Hub was shifting from side to side. The ground beneath it rippled like the sea.

No, not an earthquake. It's them. They're breaking through. They're leaving. All they needed was more time. That was all they wanted. Time to protect themselves.

Zak saw a huge, dark shadow appear on the ground under The Hub. He pulled himself closer to the gaping window and squinted against the cold. As he watched, there was a sharp *CRACK!* and a massive split opened in the ice beneath the Hub's legs. Powdery snow cascaded into it like a waterfall dropping into eternity as it tore open from one end of the Outpost to the other, a vicious zigzag snaking in both directions, separating the ground right across the bowl of the landscape.

The soldiers backed away towards Storage and watched as the crack grew like a lightning bolt tearing through the ice, heading right for The Chasm in the distance. The ground began to swell upwards. It bulged around the edges of the fissure, stretching and splitting apart. The Hub rose higher than the other modules, the tunnels creaking and groaning as they strained at the places where they connected to the buildings.

Zak heard the shouts of the men inside as the modules separated, upended, and turned over on to their sides like they were cardboard boxes. The Control Module slipped backwards, hanging over the edge of the ravine until the weight of it became too much for its fixings and it broke away from the East Tunnel and slipped into the darkness.

The Medical Station followed it, tearing away and collapsing into the abyss. Two or three seconds later there was a loud thump followed by a plume of powdery snow billowing upwards, rolling out across the landing strip and smothering the remaining soldiers. It forced its way in through the smashed window of the Storage building, exploding like a wet sneeze, coating everything in snow.

When the cloud settled, most of Outpost Zero was gone. The Hub, the whole of the East Tunnel. The West Tunnel, too, had disappeared into the newly formed ravine – only one of the living quarters remained, lying on its side at the edge of the huge split in the ground, the walls crushed inwards. The Drone Bay was far away from its original position, upturned and blasted outwards by the swarm that was now exploding from the gaping hole in the ice.

The size of it was overwhelming. Right across the length of the crevasse, as far as Zak could see, the swarm erupted from the ice like a rising curtain of shadow. Oil-slick colours shimmered through every part of it, dancing in time with the Aurora flickering in the sky over the mountains. It hummed with the clatter and buzz of countless wings, lifting further and further. Even when it was towering over the place where Outpost Zero had been, there was still no sign the swarm was close to having risen completely from its burial site, but it began to shift.

Insects started moving towards the centre of the swarm, focusing themselves into a massive column of shifting colour, growing higher and higher, turning like a vortex, a never-ending swirl that dragged the remaining insects towards it until they were all together, rising high into the glowing sky.

The only sound was the tremendous rattle of billions of tiny wings.

'An Ark.' Zak didn't even know he said it aloud. 'It's an Ark.'

Lights blinked inside the dense column of insects, erratic at first, like a fluorescent tube light coming on, flickering, flickering, then moving with more confidence. Bright yellow streaks appeared as more and more of the insects illuminated the spots on their backs, and those which were alight began to spiral upwards within the main column. More and more of them followed, thickening the spirals, making an endless cord of movement along the length of the column.

Zak couldn't look away from it. The sheer size and perfection was mesmerizing. He recalled the images he had seen when he touched the thing in the cavern and he knew what it was. It was pure life. Everything anyone knew – or had ever known – had started here, with them, and they had been waiting billions of years until they were needed again. But they had been discovered. Uncovered. Disturbed and threatened. And now they needed to find somewhere new. Somewhere safe to wait until they were needed again. Until the life here on Earth had faded and gone, and new life was required.

They were life. They were hope. They were everything.

The remaining soldiers stood on the ice with their heads back, watching the swarm become a huge sleek slab of black, with double spirals endlessly spinning upwards. It appeared to be solid now, defying all logic, simply floating above the gaping hole in the ice.

Zak felt his connection to the hive – the *Ark* – grow stronger. He felt a billion minds merging with his own. It was gentle at first; the same darkening around his vision that he had felt many times already since coming here. But the intensity of it grew and grew until, with a jolt, white-hot pain filled his body. Zak put back his head and screamed as it raged through him. It fizzed and burned like a world on fire, leaping from one cell to the next, engulfing his body, and ripping into his mind with the agony of a world of thoughts and images.

Somewhere beneath the pain and the sense of being utterly possessed, Zak had a thought of his own.

I'm dying.

But even as the idea formed, the pain stopped.

It was as if it had never been there.

Above the ice, the spirals within the column flickered and disappeared. Time had stopped. The small world of what was happening right there in that spot in Antarctica, the most isolated place on the planet, was holding its breath as it waited to see what the Ark was going to do next.

Zak's heart had time to beat three times before a stream of insects burst from the Ark as if it had grown a limb. Still connected to the main column, the limb rushed across the airstrip, over the heads of the soldiers, and burst though the Storage window.

Zak flinched from it, turning his head and closing his eyes

as the limb touched him, and insects swarmed over his body. They poured across him, finding gaps in his clothing, crawling in his hair, clattering in his ears, covering his face, smothering his mouth. He tried to move, to get away from them, but there were too many of them. Some began to shed their armour and force their way inside him. Through his ears and mouth and nose, suffocating him, and he knew he was going to–

No. I'm not going to die. They're not killing me. They're making me whole.

Zak relaxed and surrendered to the weirdest feeling he had ever experienced. The fleshy insects were inside his head, breaking down into their life-giving components. He felt them melting into his brain, their cells knitting together with his, becoming part of him. It was a soothing sensation, followed by a release of pressure, as if a splinter was being drawn out from inside him. And he knew what they were doing. They were taking away his illness. They were curing him.

When the limb of insects withdrew, the floor around Zak was littered with the discarded remains of those that had crawled inside him. Those that had *cured* him. Outside, the Ark began to glow once more, spinning faster and faster until every insect illuminated itself at once, emitting a tremendous pulse of light that flashed outwards across the ice.

Zak put his hands to his face and squeezed his eyes shut against the light that burned with incredible intensity. And then it was gone, leaving an image of the Ark burnt into his vision.

As the image began to fade, Zak forced his eyes open and looked out at where Outpost Zero had been.

The soldiers were now sprawled across the ice. Some lay like they had been frozen while making snow angels, others were bundled with their arms tucked under them. The woman in black was on her front, legs splayed as if she were a rag doll cast aside by a grumpy child.

Zak turned his eyes to the sky, but there was nothing more to see. There was no sign of the swarm that had been buried beneath Outpost Zero.

The Ark was gone. It had moved on, searching for a new place to hide and wait.

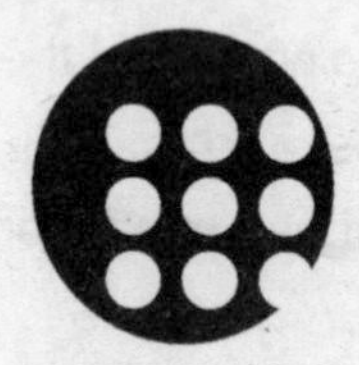

OUTPOST ZERO, ANTARCTICA
NOW

Where there there had once been a peaceful base, there was now a war zone. The ground was split in two, ragged and terrifying. Crumpled buildings were thrown aside like junk. Smoke filled the air, billowing from the burning aircraft, while flames licked at its carcass, casting an orange hue across the landing strip. The soldiers lay motionless in the snow. The ground was littered with torn metal and smouldering wreckage.

At the back of Storage, lying in a heap with the other men, women and children from Outpost Zero, were Zak's mum and dad. His sister, May.

Please let them be OK. Please let them be OK.

Fearing the worst but hoping for the best, Zak scrambled across toppled shelving units, scattering supplies in his rush to reach his family. He went to May first, despairing when he saw her skin drained of colour, her black hair dusted with broken glass and powdery snow. Her eyes were shut, and for one unimaginable moment Zak thought she was dead – that they were *all* dead. He dropped to his knees and put his ear to her chest. With a wash of relief, he heard the faint drum of her heart.

Du-dum. Du-dum. Du-dum.

It was quiet but it was definitely there.

Thank you. He sat back and turned his eyes to the ceiling as he let out his breath.

Zak moved to check on Mum and Dad, relieved that both were in the same state as his sister – their eyes were closed and they were unconscious, but they had heartbeats.

'Mmm.' The groan startled him and he sat back in surprise.

'May?' When she didn't respond, Zak shook her gently, but the best she could manage was another quiet groan. He sat with her for a while, but she didn't stir again. And as he sat, his mind drifted to the world outside Storage. The soldiers.

He left May's side and went back to the shattered window to look at the soldiers lying sprawled in the snow. He had no idea when they would wake up, but he was sure that when they did, they would be just as dangerous as before.

His family was alive. They had survived this ordeal, and he couldn't let anything else happen to them. Those soldiers were the biggest threat now. He had to deal with them. Disarm them.

Climbing back through the debris, he went to the door and slammed his fist on the button. Before it was even halfway open, he pushed through and hurried out. At the bottom of the steps, he stopped and looked down to where Sofia lay.

There were no lights – when Outpost Zero disappeared, the power module and its generators had disappeared with it – but the Aurora still rippled in the sky, and the glow of a million stars reflected from the empty insect coverings that lay on the ice around Sofia. She was surrounded by them, just as *he* had been after the insects had come to him in Storage. Had they come to Sofia too? Had they fixed her too?

Zak knelt beside her and dared to hope for the impossible. He hesitated, afraid to be wrong, and put his hands under her side to turn her over.

He put his ear to her chest and heard the best music in the world.

She was breathing. Sofia was alive. The insects had cured him, and they had given *her* life.

Zak half carried, half dragged Sofia up the stairs and into the relative warmth of Storage. He checked her heartbeat again, to be sure, and went back outside to hurry across the ice. Heading straight for the woman in black, he tugged the pistol from her holster and threw it as far away as he could. It disappeared into the snow with a crump. The grenade launcher was still clasped in her grip, so Zak forced her fingers apart and prised it from her. He slung it over his shoulder and took it with him as he jogged out towards the next body lying in the snow. Knowing they might wake at any time, Zak scrambled to free the operative of his weapons and continued on to the next soldier.

He went from one to another, and when he had relieved them all of their weapons, he stumbled towards the ravine left by the insects. He inched as close to the edge as he dared, and dropped the rifles, one by one, into the abyss.

What now?

Turning around, Zak looked across the landing strip at Storage, and understood why the insects had controlled the people from Outpost Zero. It had been to keep them safe. They had known what would happen when they finally erupted from the ice. Storage was the only building that was untouched. Everything else was either gone or destroyed; the Hub, the Medical Station, Control–

No comms. The thought jolted through him. They had no way to contact the outside world. Zak was certain that if the base had still been standing, the communications would have returned to normal now the insects were gone, but the base *wasn't* still standing. Any chance they had of contacting the outside world had disappeared into the bottomless pit that had opened in the ice.

Zak scanned the area, and his gaze came to rest on the second Osprey sitting on the landing strip.

That would be their escape. There was no other way out

of here. Dima would have to fly it.

With the idea set firmly in his mind, Zak broke into a run, crossing the landing strip as fast as he could. He was exhausted, desperate for each breath, but the thought of taking his family to safety, and leaving this place far behind, kept him going. He could even picture it in his mind; waking them up, everybody climbing into the back of the aircraft and flying away. This was it, they were finally going to–

Something grabbed at Zak's ankle and he went sprawling face first into the snow. He didn't miss a beat, though. Straight away, he clambered forward on to his hands and knees, scrambling over the ice without looking back. Only when he had crawled a few metres, did he get to his feet and turn to see what had attacked him.

The soldier was propped on his elbows, watching Zak like he couldn't work out who he was or what he was doing there. He blinked hard and shook his head, trying to get to his feet but failing. Around him, the other soldiers were beginning to stir.

'Boy.' The voice came from behind him. Quiet and muffled, but commanding. 'Boy.'

Zak spun around to see the woman in black on one knee, between him and Storage. Both her hands were on the ground as she tried to push to her feet.

'Stay where you are,' she said.

'Get lost.' Zak rushed forward as the woman tried to stand. He slammed into her as hard as he could, barging her with his shoulder, sending her sprawling. The impact of it rattled his teeth, but he didn't waste time trying to recover. If the soldiers were starting to come round, it meant everyone inside Storage probably was too. He had to get to them. He had to tell them the soldiers were unarmed. A group of nerdy scientists against highly trained soldiers didn't have the best chance, but they were smart; if they all worked together, they might be able to overcome them.

As he came close to the edge of the landing strip, though, Zak spotted something from the corner of his eye, and he twisted to see someone tumble out of the Osprey's side door.

The pilot! I forgot about the pilot!

The man struggled to his feet. He used one hand to support himself against the fuselage, while the other reached to draw the pistol from the holster secured to his thigh.

'Stop him.' The woman in black spoke again. 'Bring him down.'

Zak lowered his head and sprinted as hard as he could but managed only four long strides before something ripped through the side of his coat, below his armpit. A fraction of a second later he heard the report of a gunshot from behind him.

Blam!

He's shooting at me! Zak's mind screamed, and his body shifted into overdrive. Everything was working at once – heart and lungs, arms and legs. He was running for his life now, adrenaline flooding his body.

Blam!

This time the bullet slammed through the padding on the shoulder of his coat, grazing the surface of his skin as it passed through. The shock of it jarred Zak to the left. His legs tangled beneath him and he tripped over his own feet, sprawling on to the compacted ice of the landing strip. Shoulder burning, he crawled on as shots punched into the ground around him. He was desperate. Terrified. The pilot was disorientated, but he was starting to recover. His shots were better placed, and soon his senses would return completely. Any second now, one of those bullets was going to slam through his back, or hit his head.

Keep moving! Zak had to get into Storage before that happened. He had to keep moving.

Staying on his hands and knees, he clambered across the landing strip and into the deeper snow on the other side. The pilot had stopped firing, so Zak guessed he must have used his full magazine and was reloading the pistol. This was his chance to make a final run for it.

Ignoring the burning sensation in his right shoulder, Zak stood and risked a look back. But the pilot wasn't reloading his weapon. Instead, he was leaning into the cockpit of the aircraft. Zak had a second to register that the pilot was retrieving an assault rifle, then something hit him hard from the left.

Zak's boots left the ground and he went sprawling, snow filling his mouth and burning in his eyes. Trying to recover, he pushed to his knees, but before he could stand, an arm wrapped around his neck and dragged him hard to his feet. His head twisted, his neck strained, and he heard the woman in black speak into his ear. 'Nice try, kid.'

Footsteps crunched the ice and snow as the Osprey pilot came to meet them. The woman in black pushed Zak away, grabbed the rifle from the pilot's hands, and tucked the weapon against her shoulder. She raised it so Zak was looking up into the barrel.

'No!' He put his hands up to cover his face. 'Stop!' he pleaded. 'Don't shoot!'

So she stopped.

Zak knelt in the ice, hands covering his face, but nothing happened. No gunshot.

He lowered his hands and looked up at her.

'Leader?' The pilot looked at the woman, her face hidden by the battle helmet. 'Is something wrong?'

'I . . .' She leant forward, pointing the rifle. Zak flinched, but still she didn't shoot. 'I can't,' she said.

'Can't?' the pilot asked.

'No.'

Could it be? Zak thought. Could it be that the insects had given him something unexpected? In those moments before they left, when they smothered him, and filled him with life, maybe they had done more than just cure him. Maybe they had taken the sickness from his brain, and in its place they had given him a way to connect with other minds, the way *they* had connected with *his*. The way they had controlled the red-jackets.

So Zak concentrated like he had concentrated when he was in the wreckage of the plane, misleading the red-jackets. He stared at the woman in black, trying to put an image in her head. An image of her doing everything he told her to do. 'You won't shoot,' he said.

The woman in black paused. 'I won't shoot.'

It worked! It actually *worked!*

'You're going to put that down,' he said.

'No, I'm not,' she replied. 'I'm going to–'

'You're going to put that down,' Zak tried again, concentrating harder, imagining her obeying him.

This time, the woman in black shifted the weight of the rifle and lowered it with both hands. 'I'm going to put this down.' She dropped it into the snow.

Behind her, the other soldiers glanced at one another in confusion.

It's like a Jedi mind trick! As crazy as it seemed, that's what it was like. Zak was Obi-Wan, waving his hand and saying, 'These aren't the droids you're looking for.'

No, it's more like when Rey tells the stormtrooper to remove her restraints and drop the gun. When she's just beginning to realize what she can do.

Zak tried not to let the mixture of excitement and confusion overwhelm him. Instead, he fixed his mind on what he wanted the woman to do.

'You're going to sit on the ground,' he said.

'I'm going to sit on the ground.' The woman in black did exactly as she was told.

'All of you.' Zak imagined them all sitting down, and when he spoke the words, they all did exactly as he pictured it. They all sat down, and he turned to see Mum and Dad and May coming out of Storage, followed by Dima and all the others from Outpost Zero. Even Sofia was on her feet, flanked by her mama and papa.

'You're OK.' Zak couldn't hide his relief.

'Zak?' May asked as she ran over to him. 'What's going on? What happened?'

'I'm not completely sure.' He was overwhelmed to see them all, but didn't dare break his concentration. 'But I don't know how long this is going to last.'

'How long what's going to last?' May asked, but Mum and Dad were close on her heels, trying to wrap their arms around Zak as soon as they reached him.

He pushed them away and spoke to Dima. 'Can you fly that thing?'

Dima cast his eyes over the Osprey. 'Where did it come from? What happened to my plane?'

'Can you fly it?' Zak asked again.

Dima shrugged. 'I can fly anything.'

'Good. Get in and wait for me. All of you.'

'What on earth is going on?' Mum said. 'We're–'

'Just get in the plane. Please. All of you.'

Mum's face dropped and she blinked once. 'Of course, sweetheart, whatever you say.'

Zak didn't watch as the group made their way to the Osprey and climbed on board; he kept his eyes on the woman in black. 'You,' he said. 'Take off your helmet.'

She placed her hands on either side of the helmet and lifted it from her head. She placed it carefully on the ice beside her and stared at Zak.

She was blonde, with short hair, and an average face.

She had no distinguishing features and nothing about her appearance was remarkable. She certainly didn't look like a monster. Didn't look extraordinary in any way. She was the kind of person Zak would pass on the street and not take any notice of at all.

'Where did you come from?' Zak asked her.

'November Island. Indian Ocean.'

'Why?'

'To secure the base, secure whatever is under the ice, eliminate everyone, await further instruction.'

'Eliminate *everyone*?'

'Yes. No loose ends.'

Zak took a deep breath. 'Who sent you?'

'Phoenix.'

'What's Phoenix?'

'I don't know. I receive a message and that's it.'

Zak didn't want to hear any more. He wanted to get out of there, to get as far away as possible from these people and from Outpost Zero. 'Do you have some way to communicate with wherever you came from?'

'Yes.'

'OK.' He thought about what to tell her. 'Right. When we've gone, I want you and your men to wait five minutes,' he said. 'Actually, make that ten minutes . . . then you can go to Storage. It should be warm enough for you in there. Huddle together or something. I want you to wait ten hours before you tell anyone you're here, do you understand?'

'I understand.'

'Good.' Zak stepped back, wondering if he would still

have control when he moved away from her. How did this work? Was there a limit? How long would it last? He had a million questions, but now wasn't the time to think about them. He had to concentrate. Keep everyone safe.

'One other thing,' he said.

'Yes?'

Zak raised his voice to all the soldiers. 'When you leave here, you will all forget us. You'll forget this place. You'll forget everything that happened. You've never been here, do you understand?'

They replied as one. 'Yes. We understand.'

'Good.' Zak walked backwards a few paces, and turned around, cringing, waiting for a sudden shout, an attack or . . . but nothing happened.

As Zak climbed on board the Osprey, he looked back to see the woman in black still sitting on the ice with the rest of her surviving soldiers.

'What's going on?' Dima asked as he closed the door behind them.

'I'll explain it all later,' Zak said. 'For now, just get us out of here.'

'As you wish.' Dima secured the door and went straight to the cockpit to begin preparations for take-off.

Inside, the Osprey was packed full with the people from Outpost Zero. Stunned and confused, they were talking among themselves, trying to remember what had happened to them. Zak pushed past them and went to his mum and dad. He threw his arms around them and hugged them tight.

'What happened?' Dad asked. 'Are you all right? What's–'

'I'm fine,' Zak said. 'Actually, no, I'm *better* than fine.' He put a hand to the side of his head. 'I'm perfect.'

Then he turned to his sister. 'Let's go home.'

JANUARY ISLAND, SOUTH CHINA SEA
NOW

Inside his War Room, The Broker was struggling to stay calm.

The updated thermal satellite images showed no sign of anything remaining below the ice. Whatever those things were, they were now gone, along with most of Outpost Zero. The only remaining heat signatures came from the Storage building, the burning wreckage on the airstrip, and the remaining Osprey.

The loss of the aircraft was like pure acid in The Broker's stomach. A dense core of white-hot anger. But it wasn't the worst thing that had happened today.

There was something much worse than losing a couple of Ospreys: failure. More than anything, he hated failure.

The Broker tightened his hands into fists. His manicured fingernails dug into his palms and his knuckles turned white. He lowered his head and glared at the screens in front of him.

Some of the feeds coming in from the battle helmets worn by Lazarovich's team were dead. The screens hissed and displayed a snowstorm of nothing. These were the pilot and the operatives who had died when the base fell into the darkness of the ice. They did not concern The Broker. He was more interested in the other feeds. In particular, he was watching the feed coming in from an operative identified as 'Lewis', because Lewis had a clear view of the remaining team.

In Lewis's feed, The Broker could see the others on their knees in the snow. None of them was armed. None of them moved. None of them even turned their head; they simply knelt and stared at the Storage building.

The Broker tried to make sense of what he was seeing. Of what he had *seen*.

When Phoenix had first contacted him with the images of Outpost Zero, The Broker had expected something big. He had imagined vast pools of minerals that could be mined and sold. He imagined an archaeological discovery that would be worth millions. He imagined a new and powerful energy source. But what he had seen erupt from the ground beneath Outpost Zero was more strange and unusual than any of those things, and it had slipped out of his grasp.

He closed his eyes and took a long deep breath, trying to soothe his rising anger.

Relax.

When his breathing was under control, he opened his eyes and focused on the feed coming in from Lazarovich's helmet. The Reeves boy had told her to take it off, and she had done exactly as he instructed. It was now on the ice. The bottom part of the screen was obscured by a dusting of snow, but the rest of it showed him the remaining Osprey. Right now, the rotors were spinning as it prepared to take off.

It was uncanny, the way the Reeves boy had commanded Lazarovich. It was as if he had hypnotized her. The Broker had seen everything that happened – the battle, the rip in the ice, the collapse of Outpost Zero, the appearance of . . . what? What *had* come out of the ice? Some kind of swarm?

Whatever it was, it had touched the boy. Changed him somehow. The Broker couldn't think of any other reason why Lazarovich was so firmly under the boy's control. And he'd also seen what happened to the girl. Lazarovich had shot her dead, but she wasn't dead any more; not after those things had worked their magic.

Watching the images coming in from Lazarovich's battle helmet, The Broker saw the Osprey rise from the ground and lift out of view. He listened to the sound of the engines and imagined the aircraft climbing, turning and moving away. He waited until everything was silent, and continued to watch the operatives kneeling in the ice.

None of them moved.

With a sigh, The Broker pulled his smartphone towards him and touched his thumb to the recognition pad. When it lit up, he tapped an icon in the shape of a phoenix.

The phone rang once before Phoenix answered. 'Sir.'

'I can assume you saw everything?'

'Yes, sir. I've been trying to contact the team. I have direct comms, but there's no reply. It's like they're zombies. What did that boy do to them?'

'I don't know, but I want to find out. I want to talk to him. Track that aircraft. Find out where it goes.'

'Yes, sir.'

'And send someone to bring back Lazarovich. I can't afford to see another one of my agents go rogue.'

'Sir.'

The Broker didn't wait for anything else. He cut off the call and stood up, allowing his fury to flare with a sharp, sudden explosion. It surged through him, uncontrollable and violent. He swatted the 'World's Best Dad' mug from the table beside him. There was a *ting!* when his wedding ring struck it, and the mug shot across the War Room. It slammed into the far wall and exploded into a hundred pieces.

Before the fragments of the mug hit the ground, The Broker grabbed the table from beside him, and launched it at the wall.

The table struck the centre screen with a loud *crash!* The screen dented in the middle, and a crack flared out in both directions, running diagonally from corner to corner. As soon as the table dropped to the floor, The Broker surged forward, kicking it out of his way. He grabbed the screen with both hands, and with one powerful wrench he tore it from the wall. He lifted it over his head and brought it down hard on the floor, over and over again until the screen came apart, components spilling out and scattering across the floor. He threw the carcass aside and grabbed another screen, about to rip it from the wall and–

Knock knock.

A gentle tap at the door.

The Broker stopped.

Knock knock. 'Everything all right, Dad?' A voice outside. His son.

Still holding the screen, The Broker turned to look at the door. 'Yes, David, everything's fine. I dropped my mug. Sorry – it's the one you gave me for my birthday.'

'Oh.' There was a pause. 'Well, anyway, Mum says there's coffee and cake if you want it.'

'I'll be there in a second.' The Broker cleared his throat and let go of the screen. He dusted himself off and straightened his hair, taking a moment to calm himself before going to the door.

When he left the War Room, his son David was waiting outside.

'You sure everything's all right?' David leant to one side, trying to look into the room.

'Fine.' The Broker closed the door. There was a *click* as it locked.

'It's just . . . I thought I heard–'

'Everything's good.' The Broker ruffled his son's hair and smiled. 'Sorry about the mug.'

'It's all right,' David said. 'We'll get you another one.'

'That would be great.' The Broker put his arm around his son as they strolled through the house to join the rest of the family. 'So,' he asked. 'What kind of cake are we having?'

WEST ALLEN SCHOOL

2 WEEKS AFTER THE INCIDENT AT OUTPOST ZERO

Zak stared at the book on the table in front of him.

Jackson Jones and the Ghosts of the Antarctic.

It was the same book he had been trying to read on the plane to Outpost Zero. The same book he had been trying to read for the past two weeks, without any success. He'd only managed a few slow pages because he couldn't concentrate on anything. The events at Outpost Zero hung over him like a dark cloud. They followed him wherever he went. The world wasn't what he used to think it was. He had seen things that made him question everything. And there was something he couldn't get out of his mind. The blonde woman with the ordinary face. When he dreamt at night, he didn't dream about insect swarms, or nightmarish robots coming to life – he dreamt about her.

Zak put his hand inside his blazer and touched his right shoulder, feeling the bump of the gross scab that had formed there. He ran his fingers along it, remembering how the bullet had grazed him. A bit further to one side and it might have killed him.

Eliminate everyone, the woman had said, and every night Zak dreamt her saying those two words, speaking them without any feeling at all. Over and over he relived the moment when she had shot Sofia. And there was a name too. Phoenix. Zak wondered what it all meant. He had discussed it many times with May, and on FaceTime with Sofia, the three of them becoming close friends through their shared experience – but they hadn't come to any conclusions. The only thing Zak *was* sure of was that life could never be the same for him. How could it? His doctors had looked inside his head and confirmed that he was as healthy as a twelve-year-old boy could be. *Healthier*, in fact. They couldn't explain it, but there was no sign he had ever been ill. How strange was *that*? And there was the other thing. The way Zak could push his mind into someone else's. The way he could make them do what he told them. Zak had been thinking about that a *lot*; about what he could do with it, how he could use it.

Of course, Mum and Dad had told him never to tell anyone about it. Never to use it. Never to make someone do something they didn't want to do. That would be wrong.

But, despite everything, here he was back at school, sitting in the dining hall with his best friend, Krishna, pretending everything was the same as it had always been. Mum and Dad said it was important to get back into a routine, to be *normal*, but Zak didn't even know what that meant any more.

'You gonna finish that?'

Zak looked up from the book. Everything around him had been muffled, as if he'd been underwater, but when the voice broke through to him, it was like coming back up to the surface. The world popped back into existence – the hubbub of voices around him, the clatter of cutlery and crockery, and the jostle of other kids pushing past.

'Earth to Zak. Earth to Zak. Do you copy?'

Zak looked at his friend on the other side of the table. 'Hmm?'

'The cake,' Krishna said. 'You gonna finish it or not? 'Cause if you're not, I'll have it.'

'Seriously?'

'Yeah.'

'OK.' Zak pushed his tray across the plastic tabletop. 'Whatever.'

'Cheers.' Krishna grabbed his spoon, dug off a piece of Zak's leftover cake and stuffed it in his mouth. He chewed, swallowed hard and pointed his spoon at Zak. 'You all right?'

'Yeah, why? What do you mean?'

'I don't know, you've been a bit weird since the beginning

of term.' He shovelled in the rest of the cake and licked his spoon clean.

'Yeah, I guess. It's just . . . stuff. You know.'

Krishna looked at Zak as if he was thinking about that, then he shrugged and pushed his chair back as he stood up. 'You coming outside to play footie?'

'Dunno.' Zak put his hand on the book in front of him. 'I might go to the library. See if I can read a couple of chapters.'

Krishna rolled his eyes. 'Whatevs, nerd.'

'Later, loser,' Zak replied. He smiled and watched his friend take his tray over to the clear-up trolley and slide it into the rack. When Krishna was done, he wiped his hands down the back of his trousers and headed out of the dining hall.

As Krishna left, Zak spotted May heading in for lunch with a couple of friends. As usual, she was wearing heavy black eyeliner and her black hair was hanging over her face. The lapels of her blazer were decorated with pin badges, and she was carrying her *Evil Dead* backpack.

She was about to load her tray with today's lunch – some kind of grey meat and soggy vegetables, followed by cake and custard – when she spotted Zak. She said something to her friends before she headed over in his direction, still carrying her empty tray.

As she passed the table where Vanessa Morton-Chandler was sitting with her clones, Vanessa glanced up from her phone and muttered, 'Hold your breath, everyone, you don't want to catch anything.'

There was a beat of silence, then Vanessa's friends started to giggle.

May continued walking a couple of paces, as if she were going to ignore Vanessa, but then she stopped dead. Tray in one hand, hanging by her side, she looked up at the ceiling for a moment, then sighed heavily and turned to glare at Vanessa. 'What did you say?'

Vanessa looked May up and down with disgust. She put her head to the side and flicked her long hair back with one hand. 'Well, we don't want to catch "weird", do we?'

Her clones giggled.

'Go on, freak.' Vanessa waggled her fingers at May. 'Move along. I don't want to look at your ugly face any more.'

Zak was on his feet the moment Vanessa called his sister a 'freak'. By the time she said the word 'ugly', Zak was standing by her side.

Vanessa almost curled her lip at him. 'Go away,' she sneered.

Zak started to step forward but May stopped him. 'It's all right,' she said to him. 'I can–'

'What's *he* going to do, anyway?' Vanessa glanced at the book Zak was holding. '*Nerd* me to death?'

May looked at Vanessa and narrowed her eyes. 'I'm not scared of you,' she said. 'I've *never* been scared of you, but you *did* make me feel bad. You made me feel like I didn't matter because I don't look like you or dress like you, and I don't get invited to your parties. I didn't want to care about what you thought, or said, about me, but I did care. You know what, though? After the things I've seen and done?

Things that would probably make your stupid flouncy hair stand on end? *Now*, you're nothing to me. Your parties are nothing, your friends are nothing, your insults are nothing . . . everything about you means nothing to me. You're like a speck of dust that I can just flick away. In fact, you're not even that. I mean here . . .' May glanced around the dining hall, hardly noticing that everyone was listening, '*here*, you might be a big deal, with your friends and your hair and your skirt all rolled up, but out there, you're just another person. Same as me. No better, no worse, just different.'

May took a breath and smiled at Vanessa, who sat with her mouth open, trying to think of something to say. Before she could say anything, though, May turned on her heel. She nudged Zak and together they headed towards the dining-hall exit, leaving Vanessa sitting there, surrounded by her friends.

'You came to help me?' May said to Zak. 'For real?'

'Of course. I mean, she called you a freak, right? No one gets to call you a freak except for me.'

May stopped and glanced at him. 'Maybe you should . . . you know.'

'You mean . . .?' Zak waved a hand in front of him, like Obi-Wan Kenobi telling the stormtroopers *these aren't the droids you're looking for*. 'Really? But Mum and Dad said not to. They said we need to be normal and that–'

'Try it on me and you're dead,' May said. 'Seriously, your life would not be worth living – *literally* – but on her? Maybe just once. Something good.'

Zak grinned. 'I've got just the thing.' He went back to

Vanessa and leant close to her, concentrating hard as he spoke quietly. When he was finished, she nodded and sat perfectly still.

Vanessa kept her eyes on Zak as he walked back to his sister, and when he reached her side, Vanessa smiled at her friends as if she had just won a great battle, then she took her bowl of cake and custard, and tipped it over her head.

'Ewww.' The girls sitting either side of her scooted away faster than Zak had seen the scuttlers move in Outpost Zero. They pushed back and leant away, watching Vanessa with a growing sense of horror.

The square of chocolate cake sat on top of her head, while the gloopy custard ran down her hair on to the shoulders of her blazer.

'What are you doing?' one of her friends said.

'Gross!' said another.

A shocked silence filled the dining hall, radiating outwards as people realized what was happening, then the first person started to laugh. Followed by another and another.

But Vanessa took no notice of them. Instead, she reached up, squished the cake down on to her head and began rubbing it into her hair.

By now her friends were pushing away from the table, desperate not to be covered in cake and custard.

'I told her it was a great shampoo,' Zak whispered to May. 'Suggested she give it a try.'

'Ooh.' May faked shock. 'You bad boy. Come on, let's go.'

'What about lunch? You haven't–'

'I'm not hungry any more.' May took one last look at Vanessa washing her hair with cake and custard, then quietly left the dining hall side by side with her brother.

'Well, one thing's for sure,' May said as they left the laughter behind.

'Yeah? What's that?'

'Well, it's official now, isn't it? You're *definitely* a freak.'

ACKNOWLEDGEMENTS

When my publisher, Barry Cunningham, mentioned that he'd read about an organization that was planning to send people on a one-way trip to Mars, I was fascinated. Imagine leaving Earth knowing that you will never return! There was definitely an exciting story in that idea, so I found out as much as I could about the project to colonize Mars, and then I began to write. But once I had begun, I discovered a story nothing like the one I had expected. My story about sending people to Mars didn't even leave our own planet. Instead of heading up into the skies, I dug down into the ice and discovered that my story lay much closer to home.

But the digging wasn't easy – the ice was thick and hard – and I needed some help along the way, so I'd like to thank Barry and Rachel L for all their priceless advice, and for listening to all my strange ideas about what might be lurking beneath our feet. I'd also like to thank Claire for her most excellent editorial support. We shouldn't judge a book by its cover, but we do (tut tut!), so huge thanks to Rachel H who has been very patient and done an amazing job with the cover, and to Steve who has also worked hard on making *Below Zero* look extra cool. Thanks also to all the other brilliant Chickens who have had a hand in bringing this book to life – Kesia, Elinor, Esther, Jazz, Laura, and Sarah; you're all awesome and it's a joy to work with you!

One more thing. I'd like to take a quick moment to acknowledge my former agent Carolyn Whitaker, who died in June last year. Carolyn was an old-school agent and a formidable woman. I had never met anyone quite like her before, and probably never will again. She was honest, direct, protective, sometimes brutal, and always fun to be with. I will be ever grateful to Carolyn for everything she did to develop my career as an author, and for all the advice and support she gave me. It took me a while to find someone to take over where Carolyn left off, but I now have a new agent, Ella Kahn, who has already proved to be more than I had hoped for. Now I'm thinking about my next book, and I'm looking forward to working with the dream team of Ella and Chicken House.

That's all.

ALSO BY DAN SMITH

BIG GAME by DAN SMITH

Armed only with a bow and arrow, thirteen-year-old Oskari reluctantly sets out into the freezing wilderness of his Finnish homeland as part of an ancient trial of manhood. But instead of finding animals to hunt, he stumbles on an escape pod from a burning aeroplane: Air Force One.

Terrorists have shot down the President of the United States, and they're on their way to capture him. Even if the boy and the world's most powerful man can evade them, how can they possibly survive in the wild?

'Everything about this book is excellent. The story is fast-paced, extremely well written and is packed with unrelenting action.'

BOOK TRUST

Paperback, ISBN 978-1-909489-94-3, £6.99 • ebook, ISBN 978-1-909489-95-0, £6.99

ALSO BY DAN SMITH

BOY X by DAN SMITH

Kidnapped, Ash McCarthy wakes up on a remote tropical island. Why is he there? And how can he get home? Ash needs answers.

To escape, he must take risks. But what's more dangerous: the jungle, his captors, or the chemical injected in his veins?

'Boy X is a breathless adventure where nothing and no-one is expected. Dan Smith's pacey prose gallops along, capturing the reader and entangling us in the puzzle plot.'
THE SCOTSMAN

Paperback, ISBN 978-1-909489-04-2, £6.99 • ebook, ISBN 978-1-910655-52-8, £6.99

ALSO BY DAN SMITH

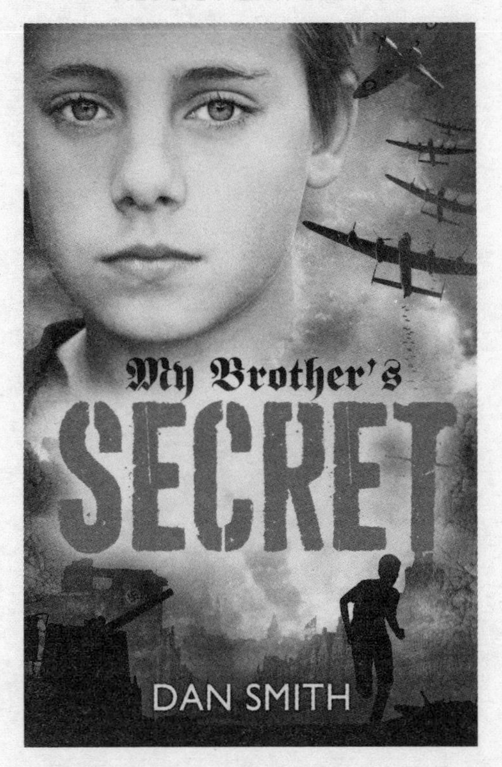

MY BROTHER'S SECRET by DAN SMITH

Twelve-year-old Karl is a good German boy. He wants his country to win the war – after all, his father has gone away to fight. But when tragedy strikes and his older brother Stefan gets into trouble, he begins to lose his faith in Hitler. Before long, he's caught up in a deadly rebellion.

'Rich in detail, this is a thought-provoking story.'
JULIA ECCLESHARE

Paperback, ISBN 978-1-909489-03-5, £6.99 • ebook, ISBN 978-1-909489-54-7, £6.99

ALSO BY DAN SMITH

MY FRIEND THE ENEMY by DAN SMITH

1941. It's wartime and when a German plane crashes in flames near Peter's home, he rushes over hoping to find something exciting to keep.

But what he finds instead is an injured young airman. He needs help, but can either of them trust the enemy?

'. . . an exciting, thought-provoking book.'
THE BOOKSELLER

Paperback, ISBN 978-1-908435-81-1, £6.99 • ebook, ISBN 978-1-909489-06-6, £6.99